STORIES OF A CHICAGO
POLICE OFFICER:
SERIOUS, HILARIOUS, UNBELIEVABLE, BUT TRUE

MURPHY

iUniverse®

STORIES OF A CHICAGO POLICE OFFICER:
SERIOUS, HILARIOUS, UNBELIEVABLE, BUT TRUE

iUniverse books may be ordered through booksellers or by contacting:

iUniverse
1663 Liberty Drive
Bloomington, IN 47403
www.iuniverse.com
1-800-Authors (1-800-288-4677)

ISBN: 978-1-4917-9173-8 (sc)
ISBN: 978-1-4917-9175-2 (hc)
ISBN: 978-1-4917-9174-5 (e)

Library of Congress Control Number: 2016904036

Print information available on the last page.

iUniverse rev. date: 03/15/2016

PREFACE

In the present climate of police bashing, I dedicated myself to write a book on what real police work is like. I describe daily events that are simple and unnoticed as well as events that would push the common man over the edge. All these stories originate with true incidents; some are embellished and others are changed to insulate those involved. None of these stories are something you will see on the news. Police work is unique in that it is a combination of all human skills and a presumption of excellence in everyone. My writings display the childlike human side of police work never seen in public and the intensely deplorable mental conditions officers are required to absorb. Judge yourself and determine if you could sustain the daily rigors of police work.

INTRODUCTION

I wrote this book with honesty and transparency about stories of police officers working the streets of Chicago. Police officers are real people: fathers, mothers, sisters and brothers. They are jacks of all trade and society demands that they be experts in all fields.

Police officers are often the whipping posts, regularly blamed for society's failures, whether they be political, social, or criminal.

Obviously, the natural relationship between police officers and the general public is adversarial. Seldom do citizens encounter a positive relationship with the local police. The mutual contact is frequently over a traffic violation, a criminal act, or some other unpromising event. Even when the officer is supporting a person, the situation is often adverse: a loved one dies, a child runs away, a dog is hit by a car. Seldom does the normal citizen have an encouraging encounter with a police officer. And, in today's social environment, everybody wants a break and few claim responsibility for their own actions.

Some police officers, a very small number, make the relationship difficult. But, the majority of police officers are devoted to protecting the public from harm. These officers are willing to don the uniform in adverse conditions on a consistent basis and put their lives on the line in order to allow the citizens to sleep in peace. These same officers run toward gun fire as citizens run for cover.

Maybe after reading about the daily antics as well as the merciless struggles, you can appreciate police officers as human beings simply trying to protect you from the dark side.

Part One

THE PATROLMAN

SEX OR LUNCH

I hate to say it, but when you have a new recruit working with you for the first couple of weeks, you treat him like he's your first puppy. You can do whatever you want with him and he won't beef. Murphy and his regular partner Dirk were informed by the captain that they would be receiving a new recruit as the third officer on the car.

The first day Murphy met Greg was a memorable one. After roll-call, they went to their assigned squad car, checked the outside for any damage, sat in the front seat, and introduced themselves. Murph immediately informed Greg that they had one rule in that car: sex or lunch. Murph stared him in the eyes and gritted his teeth to prevent his laughter. Greg glared back and with a stammering hesitation said, "I'll buy lunch." Murph smiled and said, "Great"; he put the car in gear and drove off. After an uneventful and unusually quiet eight-hour tour, they parted company after Murph's free lunch. It happened to be his regular day off the next day, but that didn't prevent Murph from calling Dirk and explaining what he had done to the new recruit. Dirk chuckled and the conversation ended. The following day Dirk and Greg were teamed up for the first time. After roll-call and vehicle inspection, Dirk explained to Greg that they had only one rule on this car: sex or lunch. Greg, with no place to hide, or anyone to turn to, replied, "Lunch." This pattern of psychological abuse went on for the remainder of the week with Greg thinking he was partnered with a couple of sexual psychopaths. After Dirk and Murph had free lunches for a week, they finally told Greg they were just screwing with him; it was all a joke. Between relief and anger, Greg was finally able to relax. To this day, twenty-eight years later when they get together, all Dirk or Murph have to say is, "Sex or lunch" and Greg goes into his "Fuck you," speech.

CLOSING OAK STREET BEACH

Every summer night in the 18th District a caravan of three-wheeled motorcycles, squad cars, and a paddy wagon would make their way south from Fullerton avenue beach toward Oak street beach. The purpose of this gathering of police was to close the public beaches at curfew. This collection of blue and whites gathered on the "rocks" at Fullerton about 11:15PM on an unusually warm May evening. Coinciding with Saturday night's later curfew, the beach closing was delayed for one hour. Being prom night, the caravan was expanded to include extra squad cars and a few more officers. This particular night they drove the rocks heading south along the beautiful Chicago skyline announcing the beach closings on the car's public announce system. Beach after beach, all was going well. As Murph slowly made his way to Oak Street, he observed a tuxedoed group of about three hundred high school kids enjoying the fresh air on prom night. Having ignored their advice to leave the beach area after a few announcements, the PA was handed over to a rookie police officer. He was instructed by their sergeant to announce that the beaches were closed and everybody had to vacate. The rookie gladly accepted his new role as mouth-piece for the Chicago Police Department. Holding the microphone a few inches from his lips, he ordered all to abandon the beach. Being a little overzealous he followed this up with, "And for those who do not immediately leave, we will lock your asses up." In reply, three hundred high school kids gave us a chorus of "Fuuck Yoouu." All the police looked at each other and burst out laughing. They told the rookie: "Go get em bud."

After a little persuasion and emphasis with the blue lights and the occasional blast of the siren, the group of partygoers slowly made their way off the beach. A rookie learned his first police lesson: threats are always a last resort.

FOUND BABY

In a broken voice, the dispatcher announced that a two-year-old baby walked out of his parents' apartment dressed in only pajamas. This occurred on a bitterly cold January morning and it was critical that somebody find him before he froze to death. Additional cars raced to the scene and quickly started a methodical search of the streets and alleys nearby the residence. Murphy assumed that if he walked out the rear door he would be in the alley nearby. Murph drove the alleys and within minutes he had the little fellow spotted, captured, and wrapped warmly in his police leather jacket. The escape artist was a little cold, but in good spirits and happy to see officer Murphy. Immediately, Murphy got on the radio and called off the search, allowing the dozen or so squad cars to return to their duties. He returned his gift-wrapped package to the waiting arms of a tearful mother.

Their follow-up investigation revealed that junior awoke and went to the back door of the apartment for some unknown reason. The door was locked but a quick turn of the knob allowed it to open. Out for a wintery stroll went the adventurous two-year-old. Mother awoke to a chilly breeze entering her bedroom and immediately notified the 911 dispatcher of the missing child. They estimated that the young man was probably only outside for a few minutes.

To this day, all Murphy has to do is close his eyes to envision the baby, illuminated in the squad's headlights, waddling from side to side, making his escape down the snow-covered alley.

HOW STUPID CAN STUPID BE?

Murphy was driving over the bridge at the Edens Expressway while patrolling the west end of the district. Traffic was slowing, and people were rubber-necking to catch a glimpse of the accident below on the expressway. The car in front of him came to an abrupt halt, blocked traffic, and stared at the scene below. Murphy allowed him to absorb the activity and, after a liberal amount of time he beeped his horn. The honk was met with the one-finger salute. Murphy initially thought his blue and white squad car was invisible, but then he realized he had just found the stupidest person in the city. Murphy flipped the switch and activated the blue lights. He tapped the siren for a couple of quick bursts and was now making a traffic stop on his one-fingered friend. While standing at his car door, Murphy realized just how incredibly stupid this fellow really was. Laying on the passenger seat were a couple of clear plastic baggies. As Murphy removed him from the car, he could see the "I screwed up" expression on Stupid's face. After he was secure, Murphy retrieved a bag of grass and another baggy of powered cocaine.

After yelling at this young man for a minute or two, Murphy realized he did not have to do anything further. This guy was grimacing in agony at the mere thought of losing his newly acquired, but not yet paid for, drugs. Murphy walked him to the nearest sewer and ordered him to empty the baggies into the manhole. He pleaded and was nearly crying when he explained he was sorry about the one-finger salute. Murphy's point was made after he disposed of Stupid's goods and allowed him to leave the scene with only a warning. He was now about two hundred dollars in debt for drugs that were making their way through the sewer system of Chicago. Murphy felt satisfied that in the future he would look before antagonizing his fellow motorists.

LONG DISTANCE CAR CHASE

While Murphy was working the midnight shift with his old friend Frank, a call of a robbery in progress was dispatched. Being too far away to make an impact, Frank and Murphy slowly headed toward the scene observing vehicles traveling the opposite direction. Visually checking all cars driving by, they were trying to get a look at the possible offender leaving the scene. A second call was soon broadcast: "Officers were now chasing the fleeing robbery offender." The chase took the main streets until the armed felon jumped the expressway attempting to elude the police procession. Frank and Murph were the furthest from the chase but they continued out of boredom.

Traveling north on the expressway and eventually finding themselves northbound on I-90, Frank and Murphy were starting to outrun they radio capabilities. The last thing they heard was the dispatcher calling all non-essential cars off the chase. Frank and Murphy looked at each other and said, "I didn't hear that, did you?"

Proceeding along at about ninety miles per hour - the fastest their car would go - they found themselves just over the Wisconsin border following hand signs from local deputies and sheriffs signaling the way. They pulled up on the outskirts of a corn field just as Chicago officers were walking a handcuffed suspect back to their squad car. The weapon was recovered as well as the robbery proceeds. A wagon was called to transport the prisoner. Great job by the Chicago Police.... almost.

During the chase through the toll gates, the Chicago cars had broken every one of the wooden toll arms but one. A Chicago sergeant was standing at the toll booths discussing the damages with a tollway supervisor when the responding wagon approached. Scooting by at about fifty miles per hour, the wagon veered from the inner lane to the outer lane and took out the last toll gate left intact. The sergeant just shook his head and completed the report needed to pay for the damages. You just can't take the kid out of police work.

A TEACHING MOMENT

While working with a recruit on a warm summer day, Murphy stopped a vehicle for expired license plates. The surrounding apartments had their windows open, catching the late afternoon breeze. The car stop went as planned, until they were back in the squad writing the citation. The offending driver approached the driver's side of the squad car and nonchalantly dropped his hand inside the open window, offering a ten-dollar bill. Looking at the recruit, Murphy nodded to the money and said, "Watch this." Murph picked up the P. A. microphone, and after a quick blast or two of the siren, he made an announcement. Murphy explained to the onlookers and those people now hanging out of the apartment windows, that the man at the driver's side window of the squad car had a ten-dollar bill in his right hand. Murphy explained that they were honest police officers and that the man was trying to bribe them into not writing him a ticket for expired plates. Murphy continued that they worked for the fine citizens watching them and they were disappointed in the briber's actions. The man withdrew his offer and shamefully shuffled back to his automobile to wait for the citation. After he received it, Murphy and the recruit left the scene with applause from the large group of onlookers that had gathered. Murphy taught the recruit that ten dollars was not worth your soul or your job. He'll remember that to the day he retires.

WHAT AN INTERESTING GRILL

The supervisors of the 17th District displayed their appreciation for the hard work and dedication of the officers working the streets by providing a lunch of hot dogs and hamburgers. Sergeant Ron placed himself in charge of the grilling. Officers working the streets could take their lunch in the rear of the station and enjoy each other's company while chowing down on a dog or burger. As Murphy was standing in line waiting for his burger, he commented on the new grill being used. The sergeant told him to look closely. Murph saw a very large, stainless steel grill and commented that it probably cost a fortune. He was informed that the new grill was actually one of the two 'abandoned dog' cages from the garage. The sergeant took it to his house, dismantled it using a blow torch, and re-assembled it using a welding torch. Voila, the 17th District's new and improved grill.

POOR, POOR RECRUIT

Officer Dave was fresh out of the Chicago Police Academy. Murphy was charged with showing Dave around and teaching him the fundamentals of street work. Lesson number one was keeping the sergeant happy. They did this by writing some parking tickets around the intersection of Lawrence and Kedzie. As Dave and Murph approached the intersection heading south on Kedzie, they were delayed by the traffic light. Murph spotted a car across the street parked at a no parking sign in front of a restaurant. Murphy instructed Dave to start writing the parking citation, and after the light turned green, they would pull across the street and he could lean out the car and place the citation on the offender's windshield.

The ticket was almost completed, the light turned green, and across the street they went. Dave exited the squad car and placed the citation on the windshield. Just as he returned to the squad car, a tactical police officer came running out of the restaurant screaming at the top of his lungs, "What the hell are you doing? We have to pay those fucking tickets. What the hell's the matter with you?" Dave had just ticketed an unmarked squad car that inadvertently parked at a no parking sign. He looked at Murphy for help. Murphy just sat in the squad car laughing. Murph let the tact officer vent a little and then stepped forward and resolved the issue. The citation was taken care of and Dave got to introduce himself to some tact officers from the district. Dave later asked him if he knew that was an unmarked squad car and Murph just smiled and shrugged. However, it's very difficult to miss those license plates that start with a big "M."

LINCOLN TOWING AND THE TRAIN

Officer Tom, Murphy's field training officer, was a very personable man with a hearty laugh. He and Murphy were handling a money disturbance at Lincoln Towing. Tom thought Murphy should handle this one alone to hone his police skills as he sat in the squad car and observed. Murphy was listening intently and allowing both sides of this disturbance to present their cases. His attention was drawn to a faint train noise in the distance. Murph was listening to the caller explain that his automobile was parked legally when it was towed and he should not have to pay the towing charge. Murph continued to hear the noise from an advancing train. As he was listening, he began to visually examine the railroad tracks outside the window, wondering how weeds can grow on working train tracks. As the other side of the dispute was being presented, Murph still heard an approaching train. He stared intently out of the window, inspecting every inch of rusted train track, attempting to figure out how a train can use a set of rusted tracks with weeds a foot or higher growing between them. He finally shut out the complainant completely and walked outside the small glass cubical to see Tom sitting in the squad car laughing hysterically. He walked over to him and discovered that Tom had taken the microphone from the public address system and was slowing rubbing it up and down his pant leg, then progressively faster and faster until it sounded exactly like a train. Experiences like this are exactly why senior officers mess with recruits.

LOCATION, LOCATION, LOCATION

The regular officer assigned to the foot post had the day off, so the sergeant needed a warm body to fill in. Murphy was assigned to Michigan and Chicago Avenues to direct traffic. It was explained to him that he should be there for the morning rush hour, then "disappear" for a couple of hours and return for the afternoon rush hour. He asked where he should go and was told, "Kid, the world's your oyster, go find your pearl." Meandering down Michigan with time to kill, Murphy turned onto Cedar Street. About mid-block he spotted an old-fashioned barbershop and decided to get a trim. As he relaxed in the chair, a burglary in progress call came out on the next street over at approximately the same address as the barber shop. Murphy rushed out the rear of the barber shop and announced on his radio that he was on the scene in the rear of the building talking to the complainant.

A gentleman had started to walk his dog, when he observed a black male climb through a rear window to his neighbor's apartment. He immediately called the police and began watching the window. Within minutes Murphy's backup arrived and they located the building manager who supplied a key to the front door. After successfully opening the door, their entry was stopped by the security chain on the inside of the door. This is an old burglar's trick. If the residents come in the front door, it allows him time to escape out the rear door. However, in this apartment, both front and rear doors emptied into the same hallway, and his entry, the bedroom window, was controlled by the police.

Breaking the chain with a swift kick, they made entry with weapons drawn. They searched the tiny apartment in a matter of seconds but to no avail. Murphy then spotted a curly head of hair crouched behind the couch. Being a smart ass he took his revolver and tapped the hair with the barrel of his .38 caliber pistol. In a fright, Murph leaped backward as a furry black cat on an end table sprang straight up. Catching his breath and trying to slow his heart rate, he still believed the culprit to be trapped in this tiny two-room apartment. The witness swore nobody escaped through the apartment window while he and his dog stood guard. Standing in the tiny front room, Murphy's eyes wandered around. They became fixed on an old style record cabinet about two feet high and four feet long. Murphy slid the thin door to the left and saw a real head of hair. He grabbed a handful and pulled the subject from the cabinet as he began swinging his arms and kicking his feet. Retaliation was instant; he was bombarded with fists by four police officers. He was "accidently" knocked unconscious. Standing over the motionless subject, an experienced officer requested a neighbor to retrieve a glass of water. Just like in the movies, the neighbor returned and handed Murphy a large glass of ice cold water. He thanked him and began to drink from the container. The senior officer reached over, grabbed the water from his hand and threw it in the old boy's face, reviving the arrestee. Many lessons were learned that day, the most important one was: it's better to be lucky than good.

SURPRISE

Murphy assisted Jack, another officer, on a disturbance call on Lawrence Avenue. A man about thirty years old had chained himself to his automobile. The problem was that a tow truck had the vehicle attached to the back of his truck and off the ground. He was towing it for being in a private parking lot when the owner came out and wrapped chains around himself and the car, causing the tow driver to contact the police. It was explained to the vehicle owner that once the vehicle is attached and raised, it cannot be returned to the owner without payment. The owner was overcome with emotion and refused to unchain himself. He was eventually placed under arrest. The chains were removed; he was handcuffed and put into the back seat of Murphy's squad car. Murph had a cage car and Officer Jack did not, so he transported the prisoner into the station. The arrestee was not a problem and went willingly. The trouble started when they arrived at the station lot.

Jack followed behind Murph into the station as was protocol. Murph parked the squad car in the first space nearest the front door. He opened the rear door and told the arrestee to exit the squad car. The arrestee tried to comply but was having great difficulty maneuvering his long legs in the short seat with the protective cage banging into his knees. Murph decided to help him. He took hold of his pants by the ankles and swung his legs around and up on the seat. Then he grabbed the guy's legs and started to pull, sliding him across the rear seat and to the door's edge. As Jack made the turn into the lot, Murph began pulling on this guy's ankles. All of a sudden something gave and Murph went flying backwards across the front of Jack's car holding this guy's prosthetic leg. As he stumbled through the parking lot, he saw this horrified expression on Jack's face. Luckily, Murph regained his balance before he fell on his ass. The guy never told him he had an artificial leg and Murphy never thought to ask. That expression on Jack's face was priceless.

A LAKE TROUT FOR MY PARTNER

Officer Murphy was finally working days in the 18th District. His partner and fishing enthusiast, Officer Ed, had the day off. Driving on the 'rocks' along the lakefront was spectacular. A beautiful warm summer day with the sounds of Lake Michigan waves crashing on the shoreline; gorgeous women with athletic bodies to be scanned; friendly smiles everywhere. What more could Murphy ask for? A fish; yes, a fish.

Murph pulled the car to a halt to admire six or seven fish weighing twenty to thirty pounds neatly laid out on the grass embankment. Fishermen stood by approvingly viewing their catch. Murph started a conversation by stating how much of an avid fisherman his partner was. He acknowledged the fishermen's ability and said his partner missed an opportunity to meet and greet these skilled fishermen. Smiling at Murph, the leader gladly offered a large fish for the taking. He expressed his high regard for Chicago police and what unselfish work they do: putting themselves in harm's way for strangers. "Take this fish to your partner," he said. And with that, he quickly wrapped a twenty-five pounder in plastic and handed it to Murph. With gratitude and a warm thank-you, Murph accepted this prized possession. He quickly drove his trophy into the district where it was placed into the refrigerator in the lockup.

The following day immediately following roll call, Murphy presented this magnificent prize to Officer Ed while explaining the procurement process. And in one simple sentence Ed offered a full explanation for the generosity. Lake Trout were illegal to possess. Salmon were legal; Lake Trout were not legal at that time of year. The trustworthy fishermen had six Salmon and one illegal Lake Trout which they conveniently got rid of.

"How the hell did I know?"

"L" ROBBERY

While they were on their way to breakfast, after a long and boring midnight shift, the dispatcher broadcasted a woman stabbed at Montrose and Cicero. Murphy and his partner Pete responded. Pulling into a gas station on the corner, they observed a woman lying on the filthy floor inside the gas station. Reporting that the incident was bona fide, they requested assistance. After determining that she was stabbed in the chest and groin, they immediately requested an ambulance and began to comfort her. The station attendant was loudly complaining about the customers having to walk around this woman to pay for their gas. He demanded that they remove her from in front of the register. Murphy went outside and shut down the gas station. Assist units arrived and blocked the entrances to the station, except for the responding emergency personnel. Murph and Pete interviewed the young lady and she explained that she was robbed at the Montrose "L" station. The person who robbed and stabbed her also stabbed the man who came to her assistance. They broadcasted all the available information and after the paper-car (squad car assigned the job) was briefed, they rushed over to the Montrose "L" station to find a man down with two stab wounds to his chest. Collecting more information, Pete broadcasted that the offenders were five black males, dressed in varying colors of sweatshirts and sweatpants. The stabber was dressed in a red jogging suit. After the stabbing, they ran south down side streets on the west side of the Kennedy Expressway. Pete and Murph assumed that they would try and get back on the "L" going south. Their hunch paid off. They drove onto the Kennedy and observed three black males standing on the Irving Park platform, one dressed in all red. Murph pulled the squad onto the inner median and while Pete broadcast their situation on the radio, Murph exited the car shouting commands to the three offenders waiting for the "L" train. They were on the far end of the platform away from the other commuters. Standing about fifty feet from them, Murph ordered them to lie down and show their hands. Ignoring his commands, they began to run toward an approaching train and a group of commuters. Fearing that they would make good on their escape on the "L" train, Murph fired a round at the stabber, missing him. A second round also missed its target. As Murph was lining up his third shot, he could see the panicked faces of at least a hundred commuters that the offender ran in front of. Murph withheld the next shot. The shots fired caused the offenders to run past the stopping "L" train and descend the stairs into the waiting hands of police responding to Pete's radio instructions. Jumping back in to the squad car, Murphy and Pete soon skid to a stop under the Irving Park "L" platform. They informed their sergeant that Murph had shot at one offender. They further explained that the two errant rounds probably struck the side of a three flat just east of the "L" station. The "shots fired" information was immediately broadcast and notifications were made. The watch commander was on his way as well as detectives and the on-duty street deputy. For Murphy, the day had just begun.

Three offenders were captured at the Irving Park "L" Station and two others were taken off the train at the Belmont stop by officers of the 14th District. Investigation revealed that the five offenders had ridden the "L" throughout the night on the north side committing seven reported robberies, all while drinking and smoking marijuana. With this last robbery, they became more brazen and almost killed two people. They had stabbed the woman deliberately in the breasts and the groin after becoming angry over how little cash she had on her. The man who had come to her rescue was taken directly into surgery, which saved his life. Three millimeters more to one side and his heart would have had a hole in it.

After the dust settled, Murph did a "walk-through" with the watch commander showing him where he was when he fired the two shots relative to where his target was. Murphy explained the necessity of choosing to use his weapon to stop the primary offender. Once on the train he could have jumped off at any time and made good on his escape. Murph explained that he refrained from taking a third shot when it became apparent that it may have endangered commuters. Furthermore, Murph described how he personally interviewed both victims and had an absolute identification of the person who committed the stabbing. Murph told him he understood that at minimum, he had an armed robbery, aggravated battery, and possibly a homicide. The sergeant and watch commander agreed with Murphy's overall assessment of the situation and declared all his actions adhered to department rules and regulations and Illinois state law.

The deputy arrived on the scene and interviewed Murphy about his actions regarding shooting at the suspect. They again did a walk-through and Murph explained the locations of the offenders compared to his vantage point. Murphy had the side of a brick apartment building as a backstop for the rounds that did not find their target. He had a personal and positive identification of the person responsible for an armed robbery and two stabbings, both victims in critical condition. He stressed that if the offender made good on his escape, there was a very good chance he would never be brought to justice. The deputy disagreed with him and out of the blue asked if Murphy shot at this offender because he was black. Murphy was stunned and speechless. With five years' experience on the police department and a couple of them including working a Chicago housing project, he was appalled at this question. The overly politically correct deputy did not believe that he had enough information on the person responsible for stabbing the two victims. The deputy initiated a U-Number, an internal investigation, on why Murph fired his weapon.

Officer Pete and all the assisting officers, including Murphy, were showered with accolades for the fine police work in assisting two critically injured robbery/aggravated battery victims. This included the quick apprehensions of five offenders who had committed about a dozen robberies throughout the night. All in all, it was very good police work.

As to the investigation, the day the deputy initiated it was the last day Murphy heard about it.

SOME THINGS YOU WANT TO FORGET

As Murphy and his partner were climbing into their squad car, the dispatcher announced a robbery offender being held by a store owner. Pulling out of the station, they turned the corner to State Street. Exiting the car, Murph made his way through the front door of a small mom-and-pop grocery store in time to observe the offender still lying on the floor. He was apparently knocked unconscious by the store owner. The owner handed the offender's pistol to the first officer on the scene while his partner rolled the offender over to handcuff him. The officer shuddered and announced with disbelief that the offender was a police officer who worked the midnight shift in their very own station. That was one hell of a way for Murphy to start his police career.

GO FOR A SWIM

In the 17th District, there was an infamous street person who would routinely get drunk and fight the police. He inevitably would be locked up and sleep it off in the comforts of a cell....until this eventful day.

Murphy was working the street when he and a couple of other cars were called into the district for transport assignments. The one available wagon was not going to be sufficient. The male lock-up had to be immediately evacuated and all prisoners transferred to the larger police area lock-up. It seemed Lenny stuffed his underwear down the toilet and flooded the entire lock-up. With a small lake for a lock-up, the decision was made to remove the prisoners for their own safety. Who would have thought that a stinky pair of underwear could cause such a commotion?

JAYNE BYRNE & CABRINI-GREEN

In 1982 found Murphy working Beat 1822 in the Cabrini-Green housing project. To his surprise he was ordered to be the lead car in the procession that held Chicago's newest mayor, Jane Byrne. Murph was taking her to her new home in one of Cabrini's high rises where she promised the citizens she would reside with her husband, Jay. Once in front of the building, Murphy stopped his squad car and a security perimeter was instantly formed around the mayor's vehicle. The curious crowds gathered to view Chicago's new leader. A news briefing immediately followed and Murph was directed by the ranking police officer on scene to place himself within the mayor's body guards. He didn't realize it at the time, but he was the only one near the mayor in a police uniform. To this day Murphy wonders if that order was intentional to make him the "canary in the coal mine" if anything happened to go wrong.

Murphy got to meet the mayor and to this day, he can say she was one of the best things that ever happened to the Chicago police department. During that one month, the people in her building received A-One protection. After a month or so, she moved back to her home and Cabrini-Green returned to its old self.

A SIMPLE FOOT CHASE

Officer Murphy was taking a ride through the park on Wilson Ave letting the gang members know he was there. The radio startled him with an excited voice shouting out directions. An apparent foot chase was taking place and Murph was half a block away. Listening intently, the chase was between the yards and over the fences running parallel to Wilson Avenue, catching an address Murph went one block east of the last reported location, turned the corner and jumped from the squad. As Murph ran to toward the fence a Hispanic male leapt over it and was charging at him. Officer Tommy was over the fence and tackled the evader while sliding across the front lawn. A short struggle was ended when the gang member got slapped with a pistol causing a small gash in the head. Tom and Murph handcuffed the subject just as the tactical lieutenant was pulling his squad to the curb. The first words from the lieutenant were "Why that man is bleeding?" Out of breath but not skipping a beat, officer Tom answered that the foot chase had taken them through the park and someone tossed a brick at him but hit the shithead instead. Murpy was in awe: talk about thinking on your feet, or in this case, while lying on the ground.

THIS IS HOW YOU DO IT

On Murphy's day off, he was bowling on the 18th District's bowling team, when someone asked him how he was going to like the 17th District. Murph was confused. His buddy informed that he had seen the transfer list and Murph was on it. Murphy called the 17th District and not only was he transferred, but he was working that night. This was all before union protection. Anyway, off to the 17th Murph went. He was assigned to work alone in a district he had never worked before. Officer Bill had also been dumped from the 18th and was the only familiar face at the midnight roll call. Along with a radio and squad car keys, Murph was handed a district map.

Soon afterward he was speeding to a call of a burglary in progress. Officer Bill announced on the radio he was in the front of the location with his partner and Murph quickly set out to the rear of the house. Bill was shouting into his radio that the offenders were running through the backyard toward the alley. Murphy spotted the first one dart across the alley and he attempted to hit the second one with the squad car, but he was too fast and made good on his alley crossing. Murph bailed from the squad and took up foot pursuit. He was closing the distance between them when they ran through a gangway blocks from the burglary scene. Once in the yard, one offender took the fence on Murph's right, while the other ran straight and started to climb that fence. With revolver in hand, Murphy let one go in the air. The burglar on the right took off like he had afterburners strapped to his ass. The other was scared and followed Murph's orders to lie prone and show his hands. Just about that time, Bill came galloping into the back yard sucking air and instantly kicked this burglar in the ribs. He handed Murphy another bullet to replace the one he expired and in a singular motion yelled at the prone burglar, "Don't ever run on me mother fucker." This was the start of a long run in the 17th district: the good, bad, and everything in between.

IT COULD HAVE BEEN REAL BAD

Officer Murphy and Officer Dick were driving down Montrose Avenue when they were flagged down by a frantic man who was shouting, "He has a gun!" Murph and Dick broadcast the information they gathered from the hysterical victim and went to the front door of a moving company. Drawing their weapons and counting "one, two, three" they rushed through the front door. Sitting at a desk just five feet inside was their offender. Dick and Murph instinctively moved right and left, all the while aiming their pistols at the seated target. In unison, they continued to shout, "Show me your hands," and after a few very, very long seconds, the offender placed his hands on top of the desk. Sitting in his lap was a cocked .45 caliber automatic. Murph's gun still trained at his head, Dick reached in and recovered the fully loaded 45. After handcuffing the subject, Murph and Dick came to the realization of just how close they came to killing this person, or even worse, being shot by him. In situations like this one, training and experience kick in and your body just seems to go on automatic pilot. You look back and try and decide how and why you made certain decisions and you realize it was all done subconsciously.

A SURPRISE FOR THE SERGEANT

Word had it that a sergeant was given a surprise gift by Murphy's partners on his day off. Dirk and George were patrolling the alleys searching for burglars when their keen eyes spotted the prize. It was quickly captured and relegated to the trunk of their squad car for proper storage and protection. When the right moment appeared, Dirk with wire in hand and George with the three-foot wide stuffed goose, made their way to the sergeant's car. Stretching their prize behind the blue light bar and strategically securing it with wire, the officers left this unique gift for their sergeant.

Nightfall came and darkness precluded the sergeant from noticing this stuffed goose affixed to his squad car. Sergeant Russ drove the squad to numerous police calls while onlookers applauded and cheered. It seemed that when in motion, the goose appeared to flap its wings. When Sergeant Russ applied the brakes, the goose was highlighted by the red brake lights emanating from the light bar.

This flying goose/squad car continued for a while until another supervisor spotted it and requested a meet with the good sergeant. The goose was set free and the sergeant started his hunt for the perpetrators. The prank was so good that Dirk and George immediately accepted responsibility. All three had a good laugh and soon were back responding to emergency calls for police service.

BE WARY OF EVERYTHING

Murphy and his recruit were patrolling the side streets when Murph pointed to a teenager carrying a large bag commonly used to tote baseball bats around. He suggested that the recruit be wary of anything and everything. They made a street stop on this very nervous looking kid. Opening the canvass bag, Murphy withdrew five long guns and a handful of pistols, all BB guns. Not exactly a bank robber's choice, but still questions needed to be answered. BB guns on the city streets are illegal. Requesting answers, the young man replied that he and his friends were going to reenact the O K Corral shootout.

Reminiscing about the famous Christmas movie's message "Shoot your eye out with that BB rifle", Murph decided to ignore this transgression. Explaining to the recruit that an arrest in that situation would probably do more harm than good. The cowboy and his weapons were allowed to move on.

On the other hand, Murphy was once himself a recruit working days in the 18th District. Driving the side streets one lazy afternoon, Murph had the shock of his life. Walking calmly down the sidewalk was a young man with a shotgun perched over his shoulder. Looking twice, and still in disbelief, Murph shouted into the radio "Man with a gun!" The address and street soon followed as Murphy abruptly curbed his squad. With gun in hand, Murphy approached the subject from behind, yelling commands to drop the weapon while aiming his revolver at his target. Startled, the young man pitched the shot gun into the grass and followed orders directing him to lay prone. Hastily handcuffing the arrestee, Murphy quickly delivered a 'slow down' on the radio.

As soon as an assist car approached, Murphy recovered the thrown weapon and secured it in the trunk of the squad car. Only then was the subject questioned as to the purpose of the shotgun. He replied that he was visiting from out of town and he was simply walking to the gun range that was located on the lake front. He was bored and while his host was working, he was going to shoot a few rounds. Where he came from people carry their guns openly and have no problems with the police.

While in the district station completing paperwork, Murphy spoke to a sergeant and they both agreed to the course of action to be taken. Seeing that there were no nefarious intentions from the gun toting young man, he would not be charged with Unlawful Use of Weapon. Instead, with his cooperation, he would voluntarily relinquish his weapon as a 'turn in' and be allowed his freedom. This agreement was satisfactory: Murph got credit for a weapon recovery and the out-of-towner kept his independence.

Police work was been described perfectly as ninety-five percent boredom and five percent sheer terror.

TROOPER NEEDS HELP

An Illinois State Trooper was conducting a traffic stop on the Edens Expressway and when it went bad, he called a 10-1. Chicago Police are his lifeline and the plea for assistance was simultaneously broadcast over various CPD radios.

Working days, Murphy activated the emergency equipment and started his bizarre journey. Racing to the closest entrance ramp, Murphy slid around the barriers and gunned the engine. Flying down the ramp attempting to reach the struggling Trooper, Murphy came to the realization that the ramp ended. There was about an eighteen inch drop-off and Murphy was air-borne before he knew it. Sparks and gravel and dust. Skidding across the empty space where a ramp was supposed to be, the squad car came to an abrupt halt. Surveying the situation, Murph realized that the state highway department was rebuilding some entrance ramps and Murphy had just found one that wasn't completed. There was a fifty-foot long gravel foundation located between freshly pored surfaces and Murphy was sitting in the middle of it. The new concrete surface was well above the front bumper of the car. Murphy quickly devised a plan of action and dragged long beams that were twelve inches wide and four inches thick. Building a ramp by stacking up a number of these, Murphy threw the car into reverse and hit the gas pedal. With a thud and a bump, he was soon propelled backwards up the entrance ramp and on his way once again to assist the trooper.

While searching for another entrance ramp, a disregard was broadcast over the radio: enough units were on the scene and the trooper was safe. Murphy pulled over to catch his breath and the dispatcher delivered more good news. A was man stabbed and the offender was chasing him down the street. Murph threw the car into gear and lights and sirens were again activated. The two blocks went by quickly and Murph was positioning his squad car between an elderly man bleeding from a neck and his attacker, still with knife in hand. Murphy jumped out and aimed his .38 at the young man, ordering him to drop the knife or meet his maker. The knife was abandoned and the eighteen-year-old boy laid flat on the sidewalk. After the boy was handcuffed and placed into the squad car, an ambulance was summoned for the father. Murph just disrupted a family domestic where the father was stabbed by the son. Superficial injuries required a couple of dozen stiches for the father.

Just then Murphy's assist car raced to the curb. With the situation under control, Officer Pat began telling Murph how he was responding to the earlier Trooper's 10-1 when he flew down the ramp and slid off the bottom. He told Murph, "Thank god someone built a ramp and I was able to drive backwards up the entrance ramp!" Murphy just looked at him and laughed.

SERGEANT GETS AMBUSHED

Police work is difficult enough and then you run into a person who has a cold-blooded hatred for the police. Murphy just started his shift in the old 18th District. It was customary for Murph to receive the most unflattering assignments because of his recruit status. Murphy was dispatched to the local hospital to guard a prisoner who woke up one day and decided to kill a Chicago police officer. After creating a barricade to block an alley, the offender called 911 and reported shots fired to the dispatcher. The 911 operator dispatched the call as shots fired in an alley where a sergeant happened to be close by. He slowly made the transition from the street to the alley, attempting to be as stealthy as a blue-and-white squad car would allow him. He drove down the alley with an ear out the window, listening intently for the sounds of danger. Squinting his eyes, he spotted something half way down the alley. Garbage cans and other debris blocked the alley. With the hair on his neck standing up, the sergeant stopped short and quickly exited his squad. Before he had time to find cover, a man suddenly appeared directly in front of him pointing a .22 caliber sawed-off rifle at his mid-section. The sergeant had drawn his revolver and with the drama of the old Wild West, he and the unknown assailant stared into each other's eyes. The sergeant fired first, striking his assailant twice. The first round struck the attacker directly in the knee and the second round found his other leg, separating the bone just above the knee. The offender was down. Recovering the rifle and scanning the yards and bushes for other assailants, the sergeant screamed out his situation over the police radio. Within seconds squad cars poured into the alley. The lone gunman was eventually loaded into an ambulance and Murphy was now guarding him at the hospital.

Now for the rest of the story: As Murph relieved the earlier police guard, he was informed that this guy had a broken bone above the knee and the other leg had a bullet lodged in the kneecap. Both his knees by now had swollen to size of watermelons. This guy was going nowhere.

Just the same, Murphy handcuffed one of his wrists to the bed rail, just to make him a little more uncomfortable. He did try to kill a Chicago police sergeant.

About a half hour after Murph started his guard duty, a male attendant came to take this arrestee to x-ray before continuing on to surgery. Chit-chatting as they walked alongside the gurney carrying the arrestee, Murph noticed that his feet were stretched over the edge of the gurney in order to make him more comfortable. Waiting for the elevator, the young attendant asked what the patient had done to get shot by the police. Murphy informed him about the ambush he set for the responding officers. Murph explained that miraculously, his .22 caliber rifle jammed, and the sergeant was able to defend himself without being harmed. The elevator doors slowly opened and without alerting Murph, the attendant pushed the gurney into the elevator and bounced the arrestee's feet off the elevator's rear wall. The screams echoed off the inside of the elevator, and Murph immediately felt sympathy pains shoot into his knees. The attendant looked at Murph and with a very calm voice, announced that it was so morally wrong for anyone to attempt to kill a police officer. After a lingering smile, the attendant pushed the button and the elevator began to move. The police do have friends out there.

GIFTS FOR THE NEW SERGEANT

There was a new sergeant in the district and Murphy had his own way of introducing himself. It was three in the morning and the district was quieting down. Murph drove past a 24-hour dinner on Kimball Ave near Lawrence Avenue that specialized in greasy foods of all kinds. The new sergeant's car was parked in front and he was inside staying warm while enjoying a cup of coffee. Murphy reckoned he would give the sergeant a gift. Murph grabbed two transvestites who worked the nearby corner and with the help of a 'slim-jim', a car opening device, put them in the back seat of the sergeant's squad car. The guys/girls were happy to be part of the prank and sat quietly waiting for the sergeant. Murph went and hid. The sergeant finally had his fill of coffee and made a beeline for his squad. He used his key to unlock his door and sat inside adjusting his seatbelt when all of a sudden the girls said hi. The sergeant almost loaded his pants. Grabbing his gun while straining his neck around, he was trying to identify who or what was in his back seat. He threw the transvestites back into the street and breathed deeply to slow his heart rate down. He was not very pleased with Murphy and Murphy stayed his distance for nights to come.

You just don't know the level of a man's sense of humor until you test it.

GOOD COP, BAD COP?

Officers Dirk and Murphy were assigned to investigate a murder in a northside park. A known gang member was lured into the park and beaten to death with baseball bats. The officers were in civilian dress and going house-to-house on Central Park Avenue, which ran adjacent to the park. They were interviewing those who would speak to the police and attempting to place the events in chronological order. A criminal investigation is akin to doing a jigsaw puzzle. Once all the pieces are in order, you can read the picture rather simply.

Murph and Dirk were making great progress when all of a sudden it came to an abrupt halt. One piece of the puzzle, a young lady, was reluctant to speak to them. She lived directly across from the hole in the fence and just down from where the body was found. It was very obvious that she knew something, but she refused to get involved in other people's business. This bullshit attitude absolutely fired up Murphy. He blasted this useless excuse for a person and explained that they were talking about a human being, not a god damn mouse. People like her were exactly what was wrong with life. Murph yelled that hopefully next time a person is brutally beaten to death; it will be her boyfriend or her father. He cursed and ranted and was eventually asked to leave by Dirk. Sitting in the squad car Murphy was steaming. Dirk returned in ten minutes with descriptions, important times, and a possible car license plate. A supplemental report was directed to the detectives investigating the murder. Their boss complimented Dirk and Murphy on their excellent police investigative skills.

To this day, only Murph and Dirk know that they weren't doing the good cop bad cop routine: Murphy actual was pissed and enjoyed lambasting this bimbo. Dirk just had the innate skill to extract the needed information. The homicide was eventually determined to be a gang hit on one of their own members. A six pack of cold beer on a hot night was the bait. Through the cut fence into the park the group went. And when they left the park, they left one short.

Some people call it good cop, bad cop. But officer Murphy just liked yelling at people.

WHAT DO YOU MEAN A DEAD END?

As a new arrival to the district, Murphy probably wasn't the best choice for this assignment. He was assigned to block traffic on Peterson Avenue after a request from the fire department to shut down all traffic while they battled a raging house fire. Murphy quickly arrived at his post and swung the squad across Peterson blocking both westbound lanes. Murph stood by his car with flashing blue lights and disposed of the vehicle traffic down the side street. After a few minutes he noticed that the traffic coming out of the side street looked very familiar. He had been sending the cars down the side street that ran into a cul-de-sac and they were returning in full force. Nobody looked very happy.

COME AND GET US

Why is it that a beautiful sunny afternoon should turn into a life-and-death struggle? The dispatcher described a Hispanic male running through La Baugh Woods with a gun. Murphy and Dirk acknowledged the assignment over the radio and were riding with lights and sirens activated. After avoiding various drivers that refused to relinquish the road to the emergency vehicle, they arrived at the entrance to the woods. Following another squad into the forest preserve grove, Dirk spotted gang members running through the baseball diamond. The squad cars split and jumped the curb, simultaneously headed directly for the man with the pistol in his hand. Coming from different directions the armed offender was forced to surrender. Now the scene got real interesting.

Two Chicago police cars were the middle of the field about twenty feet apart with a handcuffed gang member lying prone between them. Good police work, but the officers didn't realize they interrupted a gang picnic. Now surrounded by a couple hundred gang members, their arrest situation quickly turned into Custer's Last Stand. Assist cars were blocked at the narrow mouth of the preserves by groups of shitheads. The police were trapped.

The field lieutenant was outside the grove on Cicero Avenue and requested an area-wide 10-1 including city wide units in the area. Units from surrounding districts were racing to the scene with absolute urgency. A column of police cars was positioning on Cicero Avenue awaiting enough force to attempt a break through.

Seconds ticked by like minutes and a few short minutes dragged by like hours. Finally, Murphy and the others had enough. Jumping into their chariots, the four officers made a break for it with their gun-toting prize in the back seat.

With tires hurling mud and grass, the officers drove through the solid mass of thugs. Once the seriousness of the situation was displayed to the gang members, the thug wall divided like the Red Sea. Very simple: it was them or the police. Having a three thousand-pound spearhead, the officers made their way to safety. Turning onto Cicero Avenue and seeing about a dozen Chicago police cars lined up, beginning their charge was an overwhelming feeling.

Being safe and with a prisoner, Dirk and Murph headed into the district to process their gun carrying thug. All in all, things worked out well. No police were injured and a hardcore gangster was taken off the city streets.

A LOST PERSON

With longevity and seniority, common sense and respect should follow. Working beat 1722 for a while, Murphy got to know certain people on the beat and repeat callers. One caller happened to be the daughter of a man suffering with Alzheimer's. A couple of times a month, he would wander away causing great anxiety in his daughter, his sole caregiver. After Murph's first contact with the missing person, he realized that he happened to be a retired Chicago police officer. After returning him home one afternoon, Murphy stayed down on the job and drove to the closest hospital. He requested and received a plastic informational bracelet that they place on patients entering surgery. With his name, address and phone number on it, Murph drove back to retired officer's house and the daughter gratefully secured it on his wrist. The retired officer and Murph began a new routine. When the time came that he was on the loose again, if Murph could locate him, he would quickly notify the daughter because he now had her phone number. Murph would then place his missing person in the front seat of the squad car and "go on patrol." On occasion, if the radio was quiet, he would take his new partner to Dunkin' Donuts for a reminder cup. After he got a taste of "policing", Murphy would return him to his loving daughter. The daughter was elated to see the huge smile on her father's face the first time Murph and his new partner went on patrol, and Murphy received his reward of a hug from the loving daughter. Then and there, Murph realized that some of the more important things in life are small and that police time should be used wisely, and not only spent on law breakers.

MAN SHOT

The radio blared, "Man shot, 1722, it's your job. Any cars in the area to assist?" Murphy and his partner Rob raced into alley behind the 4600 block of Lawndale to find a man lying in the alley bleeding profusely from his throat. Alongside him was a sawed-off shotgun, with electric tape protecting the pistol grip handle. The still-warm weapon was quickly snatched up and placed in their trunk for safe keeping. Paramedics arrived and attempted to stabilize the man known to be a local gang leader. His condition was rapidly declining and he was immediately transported to the local hospital. They awaited the doctor's diagnosis. The emergency doctors were having a difficult time with this patient. Controlling the bleeding and stabilizing him was their first goal. He was later X-rayed, and Murph counted about sixty pellets in his throat area. Doctors here could not properly care for this gang member.

A medical helicopter was requested but denied, due to lack of visibility. A Chicago fire department ambulance was summoned and their patient was now speeding toward Cook County Hospital. Murph and Officer Rob followed with blue lights and siren. The hospital staff had been notified that a shooting victim coming in. They pulled the squad car into the police parking lot and rushed into the emergency room just as the ambulance was backing in. As the stretcher was being unloaded from the rear of the ambulance, the nurses and doctors were already reaching in, working on the desperate patient. As the ambulance crew pushed their gurney between the squeaking electric doors, as many as ten medical experts were surrounding the gunshot victim. Murph and Rob stood aside and marveled at the rhythm of the medical team that shouted commands and directions while moving from side-to-side, reaching and grabbing like one huge octopus. Every move was choreographed and purposeful. Moments later, the two doctors in charge left the patient and walked to a side wall. While removing bloody gloves, Murph overheard one exclaim, "He ain't so bad. The guy last night was a whole bunch worse."

At this point, Murph was relieved to understand that not only was this gang-banger's life saved, but as he found out later, he regained his speech about a month after the surgery. Thanks to the emergency medical staff, Cook County hospital has by far one of the finest trauma centers in the nation.

Through their subsequent investigation, Murph and Rob determined that the victim was intoxicated and was shooting the shotgun into the air. He tripped while holding it with his finger on the trigger. As he stumbled around a parked vehicle, the business end of the gun was shoved under his chin, where it discharged. They found out that their victim was stabbed in a gang fight the year before and the knife blade missed his heart by millimeters. Like the old saying goes, if it ain't your time, it ain't your time.

"DON'T TELL MOMMA TO BEAT THE KIDS"

A call was placed to 911 from a mother who allowed her eight-year-old son to break every rule under the sun. Murphy and his partner got the call as a domestic disturbance. Arriving on the scene, the mother explained that he refused to attend school. Murph responded that it is not a police matter and that it is her responsibility to educate her son in all areas of life. She continued to insist that Murphy accept professional responsibility and arrange for her son to go to school. She wanted him to scare the hell out of him. Murphy explained that he disciplines his own children and as a parent, it is her duty to instill her own form of discipline. She continued to attempt to force her parental obligations on to Murph. He eventually suggested using corporal punishment and she related that when she spanked him recently, he hit her back and she got scared. She explained her method: she struck him on the rear end with a flimsy piece of plastic race car track. He snatched it from her grasp and hit her with it.

After being at this call for over thirty minutes, Murphy was losing his patience. Trying to reason with her was like talking to a brick wall. With one last breath, Murphy explained that the kid has got to sleep. In the middle of the night, sneak into his room with a bat and crush his little fuckin head. With that, he felt his work there was finished and he left. Within minutes there was a radio request that he go see his watch commander. During this short but informative meeting, it was suggested by his captain that Murphy not tell mothers to beat their children.

THE GENTLER SIDE OF POLICE OFFICERS

Patrolling the side streets, Murphy had occasion to observe a couple of seven- or eight-year-olds playing toss. He watched them for a few moments before springing into action. You see, their throwing style was all wrong. Being a fairly good league pitcher and having had a nice throwing arm when he was young, Murph accepted the challenge. Parking the squad car and approaching the scared kids, Murph explained he meant no harm. After a few minutes of instruction, he had two future all-stars soon throwing the ball with zip.

In another softer moment in his career, Murphy watched with amazement as a very elderly woman attempted to clean the accumulated snow from her buried vehicle. With no place to park, he threw the blue lights on and left his squad in the middle of the street. Luckily, traffic was very light. Following his instructions, she sat in her vehicle while it warmed up and he removed a days' worth of white powder from atop her car. Making sure the windows were clear and that no snow would cover the brake lights, Murphy pronounced the situation safe. She thanked him and he bid her a good day.

Last in this series, Murphy was assigned to a call of a citizen needing assistance. He arrived at the location, a new condominium complex, and quickly located his caller. It seemed that she had just moved into her new condo and being an elderly widow, was confused as to what vents to open and which ones to close for the proper air flow. After spending about thirty minutes opening and closing various vents, Murph finally found an acceptable level of air flow throughout the condo. The woman thanked him and he left the condo with a warm feeling inside; after all, police work is not always gun battles and car chases.

NEIGHBORHOOD IDIOT

A drunk about forty years old would intimidate his neighbors with his German Shepherd. The man was rarely sober and had the personality of spit. Needless to say, Murphy didn't particularly care for him. As a patrolman, Murphy responded to a call of his house on fire. The fire trucks and Murphy arrived simultaneously. This drunken bust out was standing on the sidewalk in front of his house with his companion, the Shepherd.

The dog was on a leash, but was lunging at the firemen as they attempted to service the house fire. It became dangerous for the newly arriving firemen, whose attention was focused on the fire.

Murphy eventually ordered the man to remove the dog from the scene, and he refused. Murphy explained that he would be forced to shoot the dog if it injured firemen. All the while the dog was stretching his leash trying to nip the responding fire fighters. As Murph started to pull his pistol, the man came to his senses and took the dog down the alley adjacent to his house. Murphy stood in the mouth of the alley watching the firemen work while keeping a close eye on the miscreant and his dog. The fire was put out and the firemen were soaking down portions of the building, denying it a rekindle. Just as the witness with his companion meandered down the alley, an overabundance of water shot from inside the bedroom window. The jet stream hit the shithead broadside. This watery punch knocked him across the alley and bounced him off the chain link fence. Taking a few moments to regain his bearings, the dripping believer took his dog and locked it in his car. Sometimes revenge is best served wet.

TAKE A BREAK

Officer Murphy and Officer Dick responded to a routine call of a suspicious person in an apartment vestibule. They pulled up on the scene and observed a male dressed in faded blue jeans and a dirty t-shirt standing inside the doors of an apartment complex. Being about five o'clock in the evening, the officers didn't think very much of it and were just going to request identification and hopefully be done with it. After entering the vestibule they spoke to the middle-aged man and received a mumbled response. They again requested ID and received a non-compliant response. Murphy reached for the man's arm and was about to walk him outside, when he pulled back violently and the wrestling match was on. Within the four by five-foot vestibule, Murph and Dick attempted to handcuff this powerhouse. Sliding to the floor, they were a big ball of arms and legs. They had a cuff on one wrist. Using both of his arms, Murphy attempted to bend the man's free arm around his back. Dick was attempting to bend the cuffed arm around his back, but to no avail. That guy was one of the strongest men they had ever encountered in their lives. This hot July wrestling match quickly drained their strength. After a bout of squirming and twisting in this cramped sweat cage, the officers laid in a pile, staring into each other's eyes inches from each other's face. As Dick and Murph stopped to regain their strength, the offender also stopped. All three laid there in a heaping mass, with their chests heaving up and down trying to fill their lungs with oxygen. Inches from Dick, Murph whispered, "Should we call for help?" and Dick said, "Not yet."

After a short but necessary rest, they started up again. They didn't resort to striking him because the offender was not attempting to injure them. He was simply preventing them from getting both hands restrained. Using muscle against muscle, two against one, the officers still were losing. Murphy reached the radio and finally shouted "10-1," and continued their struggle. Re-energized by the sounds of sirens coming to assist them, they continued their grappling match. Within seconds the front door was violently pulled open and the offender was yanked out and handcuffed. No injuries to report, but two dirty and sweaty officers were embarrassed to have to call for assistance. The man was arrested for trespassing with signed complaints from the building owner. No additional charges were placed, simply because Dick and Murph agreed that the situation did not require any. He did not try to hurt them. He stopped when they stopped. He didn't try to escape. And it turned out he was a lost non-English speaking Latin American, visiting Chicago for the first time. He was also a crew member on an ocean-going fishing boat, which accounted for the near superhuman strength. All in all, the arrestee turned out to be a fairly good guy.

The greatest sound in the world to a police officer is the sound of sirens getting closer and closer when you're rolling around on the ground with someone. You know help is on the way and all you have to do is hold out for a few more seconds.

A QUIET DEATH

The radio was silent and the streets were lifeless. It was a very quiet night in the 17th District. Murphy was assigned a man down in the parking lot of a local bar. Murph figured he would go wake him up and head in for check off.

As he pulled up to the curb he observed an eerie scene painted by the overhead lighting. The half diamond-shaped parking lot was surrounded by a two-foot high guard rail, like those found on the expressways. Kneeling in the rear of the parking lot was a male with his pants down and bunched around his ankles. He was leaning forward resting against the rail; his neck was on the guard rail preventing him from falling over. He was as dead as a dead could be. Murph called for the CFD ambulance and notified his sergeant. He pulled his squad car to block the parking lot entrance and preserved what was now considered to be a crime scene.

Paramedics arrived only to pronounce his victim deceased. Detectives were notified and in route. The crime lab was not available so the evidence technician was dispatched to the scene for photos.

Murphy thought to himself, what a strange, strange homicide to figure out.

Detectives soon arrived and started interviewing the occupants of the bar. Witnesses confirmed that the victim had walked out the bar under his own power to urinate in the parking lot. No apparent struggle had taken place and the patrons of the bar said the deceased was friendly and had no known enemies. Robbery was ruled out as possible motive; this old drunk had no money. His pants pockets still contained many worthless personal items.

Perplexed, the investigation finally revealed that the victim was highly intoxicated and left the bar to relieve himself because the bar's bathroom was occupied. He apparently had difficulties with his zipper so he undid his pants entirely. He began to urinate on the guard rail and probably lost his balance causing him to fall forward. He struck his neck perfectly on the top of the guard rail pushing his larynx into his throat causing suffocation. With a combination of alcohol and shock, the inebriated bar fly took his last breath in the lonely parking lot.

CATCHING A BURGLAR AND GETTING REWARDED

Murphy and his partner were just leaving the rear of the station when a "burglary in-progress" call was broadcast. The location was the old Chez Paul Restaurant on Rush Street. They arrived in seconds and observed the burglar exiting the rear of the building with his arms full of proceeds. After arresting him and transporting him into the 18th District for processing, they spoke to the owner of this exclusive eatery. He invited them back for a dinner, compliments of the house, for their outstanding police work. A week later, they found themselves in uniform, sitting in the center of the dining room at Chez Paul, feasting on opulent French cuisine and sipping expensive French wine. The food was good, the wine was good, but the faces on the snobby patrons were priceless.

SHOULD HAVE NEVER
LET HIM DRIVE

Officers Pat and Murphy were patrolling the hot spots in the 17th District, and school lots and parks were high on their list. A small and very secluded park was the hangout for a group of ruffians. Not yet gang members, but harder that the normal kids, the officers kept their eyes on them. While making a visit one evening, Pat pulled the squad car off the street and onto the parkway, just short of the fire hydrant. After exiting the squad car they began to approach the would-be-hooligans when a "10-1" shattered the silence. Now, about fifteen feet from the squad, Pat and Murphy sprinted back and jumped into the car. Murphy hit the lights and siren while Pat threw it into gear. They lurched forward for a fraction of a second, and then Bam, they bounced backward. They hit the fire hydrant. Pat ran around the fire hydrant to enter the car and then forgot it was directly in front of the squad car.

The young hooligans were laughing their asses off and Pat and Murphy drove away with tails between their legs. Not everything police do turns out perfect.

ALMOST GOT HIMSELF KILLED

After leaving midnight roll call, Murphy was driving out the parking lot behind the station when he spotted a young male teenager leaning into a vehicle. Murph stopped his squad car and observed the kid pull a black pistol from under the rear seat. He quickly jumped from the car and started shouting orders to drop the weapon, while aiming his .38 caliber pistol at the kid's chest. The kid threw the gun on the grass and Murphy ordered him to place his hands on the trunk of the car. He complied. He was scared and Murphy's heart was pounding as well. Murphy reached down and recovered the pistol, and instantly realized that it was a plastic gun. Catching his breath, Murph asked him what the hell was he doing. He said he just arrived home from a family party and he returned to the dad's car to get his toy gun.

Murphy marched the kid, who was about thirteen years old, back to his house. The father came to the door and Murph explained to him what just occurred. Murphy emphasizes the fact that he could have easily shot this kid in the dark with an authentic-looking pistol in his hand. The father saw nothing wrong with his son's actions, but continued to demand why Murphy would point a pistol at his child.

After a stalemate in discussion, the father accompanied Murphy back to the station to register a complaint. Murphy's watch commander was reviewing paperwork when he interrupted. Murph explained the circumstances and the watch commander requested to see the father. Within minutes, the father was tutored in the realities of a situation like the one that just occurred. A police officer pointing a gun at his son was not a good thing, but, he understood that the scenario in place was the perfect storm for disaster: a teenager, retrieving an authentic-looking pistol from a vehicle, in the dark, behind a police station, during shift change. The father went away less angry and more relieved. Milliseconds is all it takes for a harmless act to turn tragic.

ROBBERY AT THE LOCAL ELEMENTARY SCHOOL

Murphy's peaceful November morning was thrown into chaos when the dispatcher broadcast that a robbery just occurred in front of the local elementary school. Two offenders jumped out of a vehicle in front of the school, robbed a student, and fled the scene. This was the first of three such robberies. The wanted vehicle was described as a red compact car with Wisconsin license plates. A license plate check revealed that it was taken during the commission of a robbery. The assigned beat car was directed to the school's office for the police report and calm over the radio was restored.

Murphy started a systematic search. He believed that the offenders would probably not be accustomed to Chicago and would become disoriented in the city's side streets. His hunch paid off. He was now behind the wanted car, winding down side streets and giving the dispatcher needed information to find him assistance. Seconds stretched into minutes, and eventually, with the offender in the rear seat staring at Murph, the robbers decided it was time to make a run for freedom. Murphy broadcast that he was now in full pursuit of the vehicle. They went through the intersection of Milwaukee and Addison southbound and minutes later back again northbound. The pursuit took them down the side streets on both sides of Cicero Avenue and almost ended by the railroad tracks behind the department store at six corners. The wanted vehicle was boxed in by squad cars from the 16th and 17th Districts. This is when the offender deliberately rammed a squad car to escape the blockade. Believing they needed to stop this homicidal behavior, Murphy broadsided the fleeing vehicle and with the gas pedal to the boards, pushed it sideways onto the sidewalk between two street signs. He thought they had then stopped. After a slight hesitation, the red compact ran down the street sign and escaped. Driving parallel to the vehicle, Murphy cut his wheel and forced them into the side of an empty school bus, but it miraculously careened off and again was in flight.

The normal vehicle pursuit usually lasts about one to two minutes and rarely resembles the car chases on television. This particular chase was much different. It lasted a full ten minutes per the dispatcher's 911 tapes. The chase now took everybody back across Cicero and down Irving Park. The 16th District eventually took over the chase when Murphy was forced to back down for safety's sake. The offender's vehicle broke speeds of fifty miles per hour, tailing out with a splash of sparks while running through alleys. Murphy slowed and took up a secondary position while a beat car from the 16th became the primary pursuit vehicle. He became so far behind that Murphy quit following the pursuit and ran parallel hoping to cut them off. Again his hunch paid off. Murphy was a block away driving down a one-way street when the pursuit took a 180-degree turn and was now coming directly at him. The robbers refused to give ground, nor did Murph slow down. Before a headlong crash, the vehicle jumped the curb onto the lawn. Murphy now chased it down a city block across front yards. Grass was flying and bushes were launched into the air. Eventually the wanted vehicle jumped the curb back into the street where it was met by a squad car forcing another change of direction. They were now traveling down the alley running parallel to Irving; he missed the turn in the alley, and was eventually pushed into a garage. Still not surrendering, the three offenders fled on foot. Murphy was second on the scene to assist in the capture of the driver who was trapped after fleeing up three flights of stairs in the rear of an apartment building. He was now fighting with a sergeant and after a few moments he was very forcibly subdued. The second offender was caught after a thirty-second foot chase with some of the more youthful officers. The third offender seemed to vanish into thin air. There were at least thirty police officers on foot running yard-to-yard in the block he was last seen. All the while, a young man was standing in front of his residence waving his arms at the police officer running by. He was ignored; the police were busy chasing a wanted felon and had no time to discuss whatever trivial crap was on his mind. Eventually some tired-out police officer was cornered by this fellow. All along, he was trying to tell them that the third fugitive was hiding under his front porch. All three robbery suspects were in custody. That was just the beginning.

The following are sub-stories that were born out of the above robbery and chase.

First, there was a complaint registered number obtained because of the chase. It seems that the Monday morning quarterbacks in the ivy tower (police headquarters) believed that the chase should have been terminated. Murphy's sergeant, who was responsible for monitoring the chase was supposed to terminate 'any chase if it appeared to become too dangerous.' There was the matter of a car taken in a robbery, and of the local robberies themselves. Moreover, Murphy could not justify terminating a chase when the offending vehicle rammed a squad car with intent to do physical harm to the police officers. And, finally, a letter from a vice president of a local prestigious bank (whose son was a robbery victim) thanked the Mayor of Chicago, superintendent of police, and the district commander for the police work involving the apprehension of three desperate felons from Wisconsin. Nothing ever came of the complaint.

Secondly, in the beginning of this incident, an eighth grade girl Mary Ellen, was instrumental in acquiring the original description of the vehicle involved. It seemed that Maryellen was walking to school at the same time as the robbery occurred. With all the parents dropping kids off at school, she was the only one with the awareness to pull a note pad from her school bag and take detailed notes describing the robbery offenders and the vehicle used. She then ran to the principal's office and gave him the crucial information. The principal called 911 to report the robbery and described in vivid detail the suspects and the vehicle. The timing was critically important because the faster the descriptions are broadcast over the police radio, the quicker district personnel are on the lookout for the offenders.

This act of heroism did not get ignored. About a month later, Maryellen was told by her father that she would be required to attend the CAPS meeting with him in order to learn about community loyalty. Unknown to Maryellen, the community policing sergeant and Murphy were waiting in the gymnasium of her school with about fifty grateful community members. As she and her family opened the gym doors, Maryellen was met with a thunderous round of applause and a standing ovation. The district commander presented the young lady with a beautiful plaque celebrating her courageous ability to keep calm in a very stressful situation. After a wonderful reception, Maryellen had her role as an exemplary citizen displayed to her loving family. And finally, Murph later spoke to the officer who was assigned the initial police report. He related to him, that after he arrived at the school, he was in the principal's office gathering facts for his report when the pursuit started. Attempting to hear the commotion on his police radio, he turned the volume up and was immediately surrounded by witnesses, victims, and office staff. He removed the radio from its holder and placed it on the counter where the entire group cheered on the police chase with the spirit of being at a sporting event. He mimicked the oohs and ahhs from the staff and explained to Murphy that he was amazed with the intensity and the loyalty the office staff engaged in. A loud cheer emanated from the school office with the culmination of the chase and arrests.

THE DAY ALL POLICEMEN DREAD

The call for assistance in River Park came from the Chicago Fire Department. Being just a gorgeous summer day, the call was very curious. The park was bordered on three sides by streets and on the fourth side by the Chicago River, where two branches came together. This juncture caused whirlpools and unusual currents. There was also a small damn that cascaded water about six feet down causing an eddy, not very high, but enough to cause an undercurrent that sucked all river contents to the river bed.

Unbeknownst to Murphy, this was the neighborhood fishing hole. On that particular day, about five best friends were fishing with beat up poles and dull hooks. They were pretty much just sacrificing worms from their garden.

As Murphy neared the park, he observed excitement by the rear fence. The red flashing lights of the CFD dive team caught his attention. Over the curb and across the soccer field the squad car went. Moments later when Murph exited his squad car, he recognized what the commotion was about: boys in the water. The young fishermen had cut a hole in the fence and were fishing on the slippery river bank hoping to catch a giant. With only a short three feet of space between the fence and the river's edge, the obvious took place. A youngster slipped into the rapids below and according to witnesses, hit the water and never came up. His older brother, being about nine years old, jumped in after him. Now the beautiful summer day turned to pure hell. The divers were attempting to recover two bodies from the murky fishing hole.

An ambulance was backed up and divers were in the treacherous waters with safety lines anchored by large teary-eyed firemen. The first child was dragged out of the water and handed to a fireman on the narrow ledge. He passed the lifeless body to a comrade who ran to the waiting ambulance. Another minute went by and a second diver trudged toward the shore with the second child. Murphy reached down and grabbed hold. Drawing the young boy to him, Murphy raced to the ambulance with the lifeless brother. Placing the second child in the waiting ambulance, hoping beyond hope, but fully understanding …. Two brothers died that day.

A beautiful calm picturesque scene quickly turned ugly and cruel. Two young lives lost and someone had to inform the parents. Police work.

OH NO, THERE GOES OUR CAR!

Murphy's first partner and dear departed friend, Ed, was the real deal. He was an excellent police officer and an even better individual. Ed was Murphy's field training officer in the 18th District. Ed was a large man with a larger appetite for life. They were assigned by the dispatcher to investigate the traffic congestion in the park at La Salle and Clark. They quickly determined the park was overcrowded due to the very warm summer evening. People were merely enjoying the city's outside recreational areas. After notifying their sergeant, they were instructed to block the entrance to the park from the La Salle side. They responded by swinging the squad car across the entrance and stood outside the car explaining to curious drivers that the park was overcrowded and there was no more parking. This assignment was rather pleasant, standing in the cool breeze coming off Lake Michigan. Life was good.

About twenty minutes into this plush assignment, Ed spotted a stalled vehicle on La Salle about a block east of their location. Murphy stayed at the park entrance on foot and Ed took the squad car to assist the motorist. Murphy was watching as Ed drove the squad behind the vehicle and announced over the public address system for the driver to put the car into neutral. He was going to use the squad car to push the stalled auto to the side of the road. Ed received no response. Ed now stood alongside the squad car with the PA microphone in hand attempting to shout instructions to the driver, but to no avail. Becoming discouraged, he threw the microphone back through the squad's window and started to walk toward the stalled vehicle. All of a sudden the squad car came to life and was now traveling Westbound down La Salle in reverse, driver-less. The car was following the contour of the curve of the street while Ed was walking toward the stalled vehicle. Murphy was a block away and feeling helpless. Shouting over the traffic noise was useless. Murphy grabbed his radio and shouted into it for Ed to turn around. He spun around and immediately started sprinting after their runaway police car. His hat was crooked and the night stick was slapping against his leg; he caught up with the car and dived in the open window slamming the gear shift into park. Murph soon reached the car and was standing next to a very tired and heavily breathing partner. They looked at each other and burst out laughing. Later they figured that when Ed threw the microphone back through the open squad car window, the cord wrapped around the gear shift and put the squad into reverse. Luckily, they averted a major incident by Ed's quick feet. Murphy doesn't believe he had ever shared this story with anybody before now.

WATCH WHAT YOU SAY

Murphy was working *special employment*, which is a part-time job where Chicago police officers work for the Chicago Transit Authority in uniform, riding the busses and "L" trains. The money was good and the hours matched the shift they regularly worked, so it was very convenient.

Murphy met officer Bob working *special* a year earlier and got along quiet well, so on their days off they would team up and work together.

On this particular day, they were assigned to ride the CTA bus on the near north side around the United Center. Bob jumped on a bus just after it filled with high school kids. As routine, Murphy followed behind the bus in a CTA police car. Murphy observed a commotion on the bus, and it stopped abruptly in the middle of the block. The rear door opened and out flew a kid about seventeen years old, with Bob guiding him out the door slapping him in the ass with his baton. On the sidewalk, Bob shouted a few more choice words while playing the drums on this kid's ass with his night stick. Murphy bailed from the squad and met Bob on the sidewalk. He looked at Murph, shrugged and said no problem, then told the little gang banger to get his ass in gear. The kid took off and they went back to the squad car. Bob explained that as he boarded on the front of the bus, their gang banger was staring out the rear window at the CTA police car. He was oblivious to Bob and he was bragging quite loudly that he would "Kick their ass, if those cops dared come aboard the bus." Bob overheard this, made his way to the rear of the jammed bus and tapped stupid in the back of the head to get his attention. He ordered the bus driver to curb the bus and then proceeded to embarrass this gang member by pushing him out the door with his night stick as he threw him off the bus.

After everything calmed down, Murphy and Bob had to ride another bus to make up for the one they didn't complete. They were supposed to ride a bus for five-minute minimum. Murphy swung the car one block north and immediately started trailing a bus on Warren Boulevard. Speeding in front of it, Bob jumped out the car at the next bus stop and boarded the bus. The driver pulled away from the curb. Murphy laid back and allowed the bus to go ahead of him and then he began his trailing maneuver. Within seconds the bus screeched to the curb. The rear doors opened and the same kid came flying off the bus. It seemed that the gang member had the same thought they had about catching another bus. Murphy had a difficult time not crying because he was laughing so hard.

A PLEASANT SURPRISE

On an uneventful and boring day, Murphy was working on the north end of the 18th District and responded to a call of a noise disturbance in a typically quiet apartment complex. He parked his squad car and walked up to the second-floor apartment address that was given him by the dispatcher. Murphy listened outside the door and heard only the slight sound of music. He knocked on the door and to his delight and astonishment, the door jerked open and a beautiful naked woman jumped out with her arms outstretched. His day instantly went from boring to outstanding. For what seemed like an eternity, this statuesque beauty modeled her nakedness for Murph's personal entertainment. The amused smile on this beautiful young lady changed to puzzlement, then quickly to embarrassment. The door slammed shut and Murphy stood there numb, taking inventory of what just occurred. Within seconds, the beautiful woman reopened the door, this time completely covered with a fluffy white robe. With blushing embarrassment, she explained, "My boyfriend is on the way over and I thought I would surprise him." Regaining his composure and attempting to retract his eyeballs back into his head, Murph explained the reason for his visit. She declared that there was no issue with her and that she would certainly control the volume of her music. As Murphy left the job, he realized that not all police work had to be violent and hostile. Needless to say, this beautiful young woman put a smile on that young rookie's face.

OK, WHERE'S THE CAMERA?

About three o'clock in the morning, Murph and his partner were dispatched a call to investigate a bank at Clark and Armitage. No further information was provided. Upon arriving at the bank they failed to observe any unusual activity. Murphy and his partner very cautiously exited the squad car and slowly walked around the bank. Murphy's attention was drawn to the bank night deposit window. It was propped open with bags of money sticking out; the night deposit was jammed up. The officers pulled about seven bags of business deposits from the opened door and secured them in the trunk of the squad car. After notifying their sergeant and ignoring the advice supplied to them on the radio by other officers, they requested the dispatcher appraise the bank emergency notification of the incident. Within ten minutes a bank vice president was on the scene. After verifying his identification, reluctantly Murphy opened the trunk and turned over the bags of money. With a whisper of a thank-you, the banker was gone, and so were their thoughts of vacationing in the islands.

A NERVOUS FEW MINUTES

Life is about timing. Some timing is good; some timing is not so good. This is about the latter. At the beginning of rush hour, the dispatcher described a vehicle wanted for aggravated assault. A group of gang members was driving around the 17th District pointing a gun out of the car window threatening people. About two minutes after the description was broadcast, Murphy was driving westbound on Addison trailing the vehicle. He counted four heads in the car with the two in the rear seat staring furiously at him. Murphy announced his situation on the radio and was given the "air", meaning all other officers would stay off the radio in case he needed to broadcast any emergency information. Murph broadcast his direction and informed all assist units that he would not pull the vehicle over until there was enough manpower on the scene. That plan changed almost immediately. Murphy was stopped at a red light at Pulaski, about ten cars back from the intersection, with the gang members staring at him. He knew they would start to bail and a foot chase would ensue if he didn't do something quick. Murphy shouted on the radio that he was stopping them and as he exited his squad car, Murph drew his .45 caliber semi-automatic and leaned over the hood with the occupants in his sights. Murph began to shout that he needed to see their hands or he would start shooting. After repeated demands, the four shitheads put their hands out of the windows. Murphy updated the dispatcher of the situation and he was relieved to heard sirens coming in. Murphy kept shouting commands toward the car that he needed to see their hands and now traffic was completely jammed in all directions. Seconds seemed like minutes and minutes like hours as Murph lay prone over the hood of the hot squad car. The first responding unit was flying northbound in the southbound lanes of Pulaski. They bailed out of their squad and sprinted the remaining 100 feet taking cover while approaching the vehicle. After more units arrived, they surrounded the gang members and removed them from their vehicle while a hundred rush hour travelers watched intently. After handcuffing their gang, Murphy quickly searched the vehicle and held up a loaded .38 caliber pistol for the captive audience to see. They seemed to understand the hold up and they began applauding the actions of the police. The on-scene officers quickly removed their arrestees and relocated the vehicle. After a few minutes of traffic control, the appreciative audience was once again on their way home in Chicago's rush-hour traffic.

PIGEONS, BUT IT'S STILL NOT RIGHT

Finally accruing enough seniority to work a beat car on days, Murphy mounted up and off he went. Before he had time to grab his morning cup of java, the dispatcher gave him an unusual job: "Check on the pigeons under a viaduct." Murphy asked if there was any additional information about this request and the dispatcher said that was all she had. Being curious, Murph headed directly to the job to view an amazing sight. It looked like General Custer's Little Big Horn massacre, but with pigeons. There must have been two hundred bundles of feathers covering the street. The sidewalks were virtually impassable with the tiny murdered bodies of our flying friends. Murphy relayed this information to the dispatcher and she requested Streets and Sanitation to send a crew out to collect the pigeon carcasses.

Not really wanting to examine the dead birds closely, Murphy had no clue as for the cause of death. Streets and Sanitation came and cleaned up the area and restored it to normal. Murphy coded the job to the dispatcher and returned to his duties of fetching his morning coffee. For the next few days word of the unusual massacre made its way throughout the district. Through the grapevine, Murphy finally received the true story about the unusual pigeon die-off. It seems that there were a very bored couple of midnight police officers, who happened to bring pellet rifles to work one night. They took target practice throughout the night…. Even if you're not a fan of pigeons, you have to have some compassion for those birds.

FREE ADVICE

Did you ever know that person who asks for advice and doesn't like what you say, so they re-frame the same question over and over again in a slightly different way, believing eventually you will say what they want to hear? Here is Murphy's version of that lady.

While waiting to meet his wife where she worked, a woman walked up to Murph and asked if he was a police officer. She knew he was, so Murphy replied "Yes." She recounted an issue with her neighbor. The eighty-four-year-old woman living next to this woman had the audacity to put her sprinkler on and it shoots water across the sidewalk. Momma's little girl cannot ride her tricycle on the sidewalk in that direction because she was in fear of getting wet. Murphy applauded the civic-minded neighbor for not only watering her own grass, but the city's side as well. Momma said that was wrong and the woman should stop watering simply because her daughter cannot ride freely on the city sidewalk. She wanted the old woman to stop watering the grasses and allow her daughter freedom to ride her tricycle. Murphy suggested that the girl ride under the falling water as they did as youngsters. He suggested the girl time the falling water and ride around it. He suggested that the girl ride the other way down the block. All rational solutions were rejected. This woman's annoying persistence eventually got the better of him. After wasting time that he will never get back, Murphy called her close and whispered that if she really wanted to end this violation, he could give her a final solution. She leaned in closely and Murph explained that the violator is old and more than likely in need of an afternoon nap. He suggested, on a warm afternoon, she climb through the window with a butcher knife and cut the old woman's fuckin throat while she slept. She finally left Murphy alone.

THINGS BORED POLICE OFFICERS DO

It had to be 4:00 in the morning when over the radio came an unusual request for officer Murphy to check his personal car. This message bypassed the dispatcher and was broadcast on the mobile, from car to car, by an unknown police officer. When Murph came to work, he parked his personal vehicle in the parking lot across the alley from the station facing Chicago Avenue. With a break in the action, Murph drove by his car in time to see a three-foot high pink elephant sitting in the driver's seat peering over the steering wheel. When policemen get bored, they do the strangest things.

An evidence technician used to park in his favorite restaurant parking lot. Working midnights, sometimes he would get there before the restaurant opened and rest his eyes a few minutes before catching breakfast. One time while he was resting his eyes, Murph and Officer Pat tied helium balloons to his bumpers and mirrors. He awoke to thinking he was in a Walt Disney movie. Another time, the same technician was in the restaurant having his breakfast when Murph and another officer filled his squad car with day-old bread and rolls they got from a bakery.

I won't even explain how it feels when somebody puts a big gob of Vaseline under the door handle of the squad car and you….

Officers Dirk and Murphy finished roll call and jumped into their squad car. Being chilly outside, Murph turned on the heater and kicked the fan on high. Instantly, both Dirk and Murph slid out of the car. Someone had squirted pepper spray into the vents. When the heat and the fan kicked on, a burst of pepper spray attacked the officer's senses. Eyes watered and the sneezing started. The car was not operational. Driving the car with windows open and no heat, they got the car to the area garage and exchanged it for another police chariot. The mechanics at the garage simply disconnected the battery and opened all windows and doors, propped a fan inside and let it air out for twenty-four hours.

Playing practical jokes on one another often took the edge of the gruesome things they saw. If by chance they didn't blow some steam off, the psychiatric wards and funeral parlors would be filled with police officers.

WHAT'S THAT NOISE?

At about 3:30 in the morning, there was a foot chase in progress. A bad guy armed with a pistol was running through rear yards, hurdling fences like a gazelle. Officers were running parallel with him in the front yards while Murphy and another group of police were doing the same in the alley. It was a very hot August night and you could cut the humidity with a knife. With sweat dripping off their foreheads, they took up position behind a tall wooden fence in the alley. Thinking they had the bad guy trapped in a yard, Murphy quickly jumped the fence and observed the side door of the garage wide open. He was pleased to think that he would have this shithead in cuffs in a matter of seconds. With revolver in one hand and a flashlight in the other, Murphy cautiously made his way to the door. Standing sideways to present a smaller target, Murphy simultaneously pointed his gun and flashlight into the darkness. He quickly swung into the garage to find perfect emptiness. He was attempting to evaluate what he saw when he heard the sounds of movement coming from the rear of the house, as though someone was heading in his direction. Murph instantly visualized firmly planting his revolver across the bridge of the offender's nose as he was running past. With flashlight in his left hand and pistol in the right, Murphy timed his approach. He stepped out of the garage with his left foot first, with his right armed cocked sideways prepared to slap stupid in the face in with his Smith and Wesson. Instead of seeing the offender coming at him, Murphy saw two huge German Shepherds in full gallop. He reversed his field and began his exit for the six-foot wooden fence. At a sprinter's pace, Murph covered the fifteen feet in three frightening steps and lunged at the lower frame of the fence. Luckily, he caught enough of the two-by-four bracing to propel himself over the top of the fence. His flashlight was surrendered to the canines as his right hand still clutched his pistol. Murphy flipped upside down over the top of the fence, while the jaws of one of his canine pursuers grazed the heel of his right shoe.

Landing in one piece in the alley, Murphy spotted the owner standing on the porch directing orders to his canine army of two. Murphy started screaming at the top of his lungs about how he was going to kill this son-of-a-bitch and shoot his friggin dogs. In a matter of seconds, Murphy rifled off every evil name he could conjure up.

The owner realized his error and that they were the police; he stated he meant no harm. He immediately called off his dogs and Murphy re-examined his position. After calming down and explaining their midnight interruption, Murphy realized the owner's actions were not only acceptable, but appropriate. They parted ways on a mutually respectable level and they quickly caught their gun toting shithead a few doors away. While Murphy was dealing with the canine, the offender slipped over the fence into the next yard. Officers, ever so vigilant, located him hiding under a large bush. One more gun off the street.

A VICIOUS HOME INVASION

Sergeant Murphy responded to the call of a home invasion just occurred in the 16th District. He entered the kitchen area to find an elderly woman badly beaten and in dire need of medical attention. A Chicago Fire Department ambulance was requested as Murphy and a female police officer tried to comfort this woman. Remarkably she was more concerned about the husband who was in the bedroom then her own injuries. Sadly to say, this gentleman was deceased when Murphy checked his condition. This information was withheld from the mentally fragile woman until the paramedics arrived on scene. They would deliver the horrifying news as well as the medical care to sustain her physically but more importantly, they would be able to attend to her mental well-being.

As more assisting units arrived on scene, the entire house was cordoned off and declared a crime scene; admittance was restricted. Murphy explained to the arriving paramedics that the husband was already dead and they needed to pronounce him as such, but without dragging their equipment bags into the bedroom. The female victim was seated in the kitchen and while one paramedic attended to her wounds, the second paramedic tip-toed into the ransacked bedroom toward the body lying face up on the bed. Feet on the floor and upper torso laying across the bed, this poor man was beaten to death by home invaders intent on stealing his valuables. It appeared that he was dragged into the bedroom and forced to reveal his hiding places. One offender probably sat on the chest while administering a beating. The victim, being elderly and fragile, soon succumbed to the vicious pounding.

The wife was secluded in the kitchen and was also administered a terrible beating by a member of the robbery crew. Fortunately for her, their key focus was placed on her husband, allowing her to survive. Detectives were soon arriving and the paramedics removed the old woman to the hospital, where she was immediately transferred to the intensive care unit.

The mobile crime lab was summoned and soon was collecting vital evidence. Photos, fingerprints, blood samples and blood smears were cataloged. Tool markings from the entry point were examined and photographed. After processing the deceased, removal was authorized and the wagon team gingerly collected the old man and delivered his battered body to the morgue.

After hours of evidence gathering, the officers guarding the crime scene eventually placed coroner seals on the front and rear doors, securing the crime scene, and were finally relieved to go home.

A more violent and brutal crime scene is not remembered by Sergeant Murphy. Shootings, stabbings and various other heartless murders are all part of police work, but this incident will register as the most unnecessary and repugnant murder he has been associated with. No arrests have been made as of this writing.

WHAT CRUELTY REALLY IS!

Teamed up on the wagon with an old timer in the north side district, Murphy was sitting in McDonald's eating breakfast at five in the morning. The radio broadcast of a rape in progress broke the morning silence and moments later the blare of police sirens woke the neighborhood from a quiet sleep. Officers responding to the scene of the rape had captured the offender after a foot pursuit across the roof tops. Murphy and his partner pulled the wagon up in time for the arresting officers to march the subject toward their transport vehicle. Out of the blue, a young police officer ran up and started to kick the living shit out of the prisoner. With the assistance of other officers on the scene, they eventually pulled and dragged the officer away and placed the arrestee safely into the wagon. Moments later, they came to understand the reason for the attack. This young officer, who was married and with two young children was on the rooftops collecting evidence immediately after the foot chase. Under a stairwell, on the rooftop within feet of where the arrestee surrendered, the young officer found the rape victim's four year-old son, lying in a pool of blood, decapitated.

The investigation later revealed that the arrestee had ingested a large dose of PCP, an animal tranquilizer. During a home invasion, he continually raped this poor woman throughout the night. She was eventually able to flee the apartment and contact 911 reporting the criminal abuse. The offender, hearing the approaching police sirens, apparently climbed out the window onto the roof, taking the child with, along with a kitchen knife. In a moment of psychopathic rage, he cut the boy's throat to the degree of decapitating him; he then left the boy's body under a set of rooftop stairs.

Murphy later visited this offender in the lockup just to see what kind of individual could do something so heinous in such a casual manner. The arrestee was so far out of reality that he didn't even acknowledge Murphy's presence.

He was later tried, convicted, and sentenced to death. Many years afterwards, while sitting at a bar sipping a cold beer, people stared and wondered why Murphy was celebrating the announcement on television news of a man being put to death by lethal injection.

MURDER VICTIM CAME IN SECOND

Brand new to the district, Murphy responded to a call about a suspicious car, curious to see if he could find it. Tucked away on Kilpatrick Street abutting the railroad tracks, Murphy spotted the car. Other officers had already investigated and notified the proper units, detectives, sergeant, and field lieutenant, and crime lab. Sitting in the driver's seat was a man with a gunshot wound to the forehead. A second wound with burn marks was to the temple. This man was dead. Looking closely, his right hand gripped a two shot derringer resting halfway in his coat pocket. Whatever the argument was about, he came in second place. There was speculation about a dope deal. Another about an outfit hit. Whatever the story, the man was dead and nobody has been arrested as of this writing.

RESPECT THE ELDERLY

Being in the 17th District for about a year, Murphy had the pleasure of knowing some very good police officers. This particular night he was partnered up with one, officer Tom. The night was going smoothly when about two in the morning, they responded to a noise complaint. The apartment given was on the second floor of a retirement building. Very unusual. As Murph and Tom walked the stairs they were met by a small group of elderly men and women who complained the noise from the same apartment was an ongoing issue. Other police had come and gone with no satisfaction. The apartment was occupied by a young man who abused alcohol and drugs and was allowed the live there through a government program. Murph knocked on the door to no avail. Tom pounded on the thick wooden door with his night stick. Eventually the door opened and standing there was a drugged up twenty-five year old, long hair and minus a shirt. It was explained that the music must be turned down due to the complaint of his neighbors. He turned the music down and the officers left. Not even driving two blocks away, they were summoned back. The music seemed louder than before. Same drill, Tom pounded on the door with his oak night stick. The druggy answered the door and was again instructed to turn the music off. The job was barely coded when the third call was dispatched. Noise complaint, same location, same person. Tom and Murph climbed the stairs the third time in less than thirty minutes and were met by an even larger group of seniors. They begged and pleaded for quiet. Tom repeatedly bounced his night stick off the door. The door opened and Tom hit this idiot between the eyes with a hammer-like fist. Onto his back he went and skidded across the wooden floor bumping his head on the table leg. Tom stepped over him and reaching the stereo, started ripping out cables and wires. Satisfied the stereo was inoperable; Tom turned his attention toward the idiot now standing wobbly at his side. Tom grabbed him by the throat and explained very slowly and deliberately, that if the police were called back that night, there would be absolute hell to pay, and he would be the one paying that bill. Murph and Tom left to the applause and newly acquired admiration of the gang of elderly. No further calls for service came from the apartment complex the remainder of that night.

DON'T THROW THE BABY

Murphy, with about four years of experience under his belt, responded to a call of a domestic disturbance. He pulled up behind the sergeant's car and ran up the three flights of stairs. Ushered through the open apartment door to the balcony, he now observed the problem in full force. The sergeant was pleading with a young body builder to surrender his infant child. The muscled out father was dangling the infant over the edge of the balcony, threatening to drop the child to his death. Visually examining the area they had to work in, Murphy realized a sick feeling in the pit of his stomach. On one nearby chair, he observed a set of weights with over two hundred pounds on it. The apartment was in disarray and beer cans littered the floor. All the while the father was shouting at the sergeant, demanding that the squad cars be removed from the front of the apartment complex. Orders were given and all cars were removed with the exception of Murphy's. Now Murphy awkwardly stood by the sergeant he had yet been introduced to. He positioned himself in the cold air of the balcony perched thirty feet above ground. Murphy witnessed the sergeant's appeal to the fatherly instincts and the request for the child's well-being. Within a blink of an eye, the stressed out father tossed to baby to the waiting arms of the sergeant and rushed at Murphy with arms extended screaming, "Cuff me!" Murph withdrew his handcuffs and nervously, cautiously, and hurriedly handcuffed the deranged father. Murph was scared to death.

The infant was returned safely to the mother and the father was taken to the local hospital for psychiatric care.

When the stress levels were finally lowered, Murphy and the sergeant introduced themselves. Then Murph asked the question that was lingering. "Why would you choose me to stay with you when we have never met? How did you know you could trust me in such a crazy situation?" The sergeant replied that he had worked with Murphy's father years earlier and if Murphy was anything like his father, he could be trusted in such a moment. Murphy accepted the compliment and a friendship was forged.

HE PAYS MY SALARY

Murphy was minding his own business when a car blew a red light and almost ruined his day by broadsiding him. Murph flipped on the Mars lights and within minutes he was speaking with a very demanding motorist. According to him, he pays Murph's salary. The reason for the traffic stop has no validity in their conversation according to him. He pays Murphy's salary and Murphy should be eternally grateful. Murphy should display his gratefulness by not writing this asshole a citation for blowing a red light and almost broadsiding him. Murphy walked back to the squad car and sat back down. Now, generally he only writes citations to every fourth or fifth stop that he makes. Tickets were never high on his priority list of police work. Normally, people Murphy stops are allowed to talk themselves into receiving a ticket, just like his paycheck-paying friend was doing.

While scratching out a hundred-dollar citation, Murphy watched him scream and curse. Murph mustered his best facial expression and approached the vehicle. As the driver rolled down the window, Murphy deliberately began to chuckle. He demanded to know why Murphy was laughing. Murph explained that he pays his salary; therefore, he was actually paying Murphy to write him a hundred dollar ticket. Immediately, Murph handed him the ticket and retreated before he fully comprehended what was just said.

Loudly cursing, he sat in the car reading his new temporary driver's license as Murphy drove past, giving him that silly cocked wrist, flutter-finger wave, garnished with a ninety-five cent smile.

MEETING AN OLD FRIEND

Officers Murphy and Julie were patrolling the south end of the 17th District, when they passed an alley and something caught Murphy's eye. He put the Ford in reverse and backed up to get a clearer view. They observed a young man straddling an elderly woman lying outside a garage about halfway down the alley. The man spotted them and fled as they raced into the alley. The officers momentarily spoke to the woman who shouted that she had just been attacked and robbed. Julie called for an ambulance and they pursued the offender as he sped away in his rust bucket. After making a few turns up and down side streets, the offender jumped out of his moving vehicle as it drove up the curb and struck a tree. Driving past the smoking vehicle, Murphy stayed parallel to the fleeing felon. He shouted commands to stop, and then he took two shots out the squad car window narrowly missing his moving target. Trying to avoid Murphy's next shot, the robber fled between two houses and Murph bailed from the squad in foot pursuit. Julie was calling for assistance and was busy with the offender's smoking vehicle that was now halfway up a tree. Murphy chased a slow-moving crook into a backyard. Trapped by a tall fence, the offender abruptly turned one hundred and eighty degrees and raced back toward Murph. Murphy immediately froze and took up a shooting stance, aiming his .38 caliber at the robber's chest, while inviting him to keep coming. He decided against that move and dropped to his knees on the soggy grass. Now handcuffed and walking back to the squad car, Murphy finally recognized his arrestee. The fleeing felon and Murphy new each other at a much younger age. Murphy went on to high school and the lady-robber went into the Navy. A name check revealed he was dishonorably discharged from the Navy for robbing women in his off-time. He also served time in the penitentiary for similar criminal activity.

Thankfully, the victim wasn't seriously injured and Murph's old school chum pleaded guilty. He was again housed on the taxpayer's dime back in the familiarity of the penitentiary.

DEALING WITH A HAPPY DUI

I believe that if you ask any police officer, the majority will say arresting a drunk driver is the worst assignment you can get. This day was different. Traveling eastbound on Irving Park, traffic started to back up and the cars began to slow to a snail's pace. Murphy swerved around traffic until he was right behind the problem. An apparently drunk driver was veering from lane to lane, preventing any normal driver from passing. Murphy stayed behind his subject and they both stopped at a red light. As the light turned green, Murphy activated the lights and siren and the vehicle reluctantly pulled to the curb. Murphy positioned his squad car in such a manner that he would not get hit by any oncoming vehicles, and he started walking toward the vehicle. As Murph got about ten feet away the driver's door opened and out came the obliterated driver. Murph reached him just as his second foot landed on the street. With that, the driver spun around like a top, balanced on his heels, he fell backwards into traffic. Murphy lunged with both arms extended and caught him in his arms like a dance move. With the drunk driver resting firmly in Murphy's embrace, he looked up and smiled and said, "Nice catch." After Murph finally stopped laughing, he gave his bleary-eyed driver a ride home in the back seat of his squad car.

UNCLE PAUL AND MURPHY CATCH SOME BAD GUYS

It's often said that police work is ninety-five percent boredom and five percent sheer terror. Murphy's wife's uncle Paul was in his mid-eighties, retired and living in the area that Murph patrolled in the 17th District. One boring day, already filled with coffee and riding around aimlessly, Murphy monitored a radio broadcast of two white guys who just robbed a store. Armed with pistols, they were making good their escape driving a blue Chevy. Lucky for Murph, he was right behind them driving east on Addison. They turned and drove up and down the side streets attempting to blend in, while Murphy was following them broadcasting their direction on the police radio. Murph was waiting for backup units to get close before he stopped them because he didn't want a car chase if he could avoid it. Seconds went by like an eternity, right and left, up and down the side streets. Murphy decided to make the stop at the next intersection so his assist cars can come in from all four directions. He activated the lights and siren; the car hesitantly pulled to the curb. Murphy broadcast his final location on the police radio. Murph immediately drew his weapon, exited the squad car and took cover behind the engine block of his vehicle. With PA microphone in hand, Murphy was shouting to the occupants of the car that they had to put their hands out the windows or he would start shooting. He heard the welcoming sounds of the police sirens getting closer. He also heard someone shouting, "Murph, Murph, over here, it's Uncle Paul!" Crouched down, trying to be as small as he could be, he saw Uncle Paul walking toward him, begging to be recognized. The scene was totally chaotic. Murphy was screaming at the bad guys that he was going to kill them if they didn't put their hands out of the car windows. Then he was shouting at Uncle Paul to get back and take cover. Murphy understood that his assist cars were flying in to help him and they wouldn't be overly selective in whom they run over to protect another police officer. Finally, after what seemed like eternity, the first back-up car screeched to a halt. After removing the two occupants from the vehicle, they secured two loaded pistols and recovered the proceeds from the robbery. Murph then turned his attention to Uncle Paul, who was absolutely thrilled about what he had just witnessed. He was sporting a smile from ear to ear. Murphy explained what just occurred and Uncle Paul was ecstatic to be involved in apprehending two armed robbers.

The story gets better. About a month later, Murphy and his wife arrived at a family function and Murphy noticed a large group of relatives circled around Uncle Paul. He grabbed a cold drink and walked over in time to overhear Uncle Paul explain how, "He and Murphy caught these sticks up guys." For years, that story was repeated at nearly every family function. Uncle Paul was Murphy's first backup on the scene.

CALL GIRLS AND A TRANSPORT

Being very new to the district and police work itself, no supervisor seemed to know what to do with Murphy. All he wanted to do was real police work. With that said, Murphy found himself working the boring wagon. But his day would soon get better with an assignment on Michigan Avenue. Murphy and his partner were called to transport high-priced call girls that a very famous 18th District vice officer had just arrested. These were not the typical street hookers, they charge more for an hour's pleasure than police officers made in a day. Murphy pulled in the alley behind one of the more prominent hotels waiting for the girls. Then, in a single line, out walked some of the most beautiful ladies of the night that he had ever seen. Murph's job was simply to be there and look authoritarian as the vice officer walked the girls from the doorway to wagon. To this day, he doesn't know if he was set up or not, but as Murphy was walking with one of the most beautiful woman he ever laid eyes on, she seductively wrapped her arm around his arm. She gazed lovingly into his youthful eyes and inquired why they couldn't just leave together and have an afternoon of pleasure and delight. A thousand thoughts surged through his mind. After regaining his composure, Murphy reluctantly untangled her warm and delicate arm from his and assisted her in entering the wagon. Murphy knew it could never happen, but he could daydream.

THE DEATH OF A LOCAL BUSINESS HERO

As a patrolman, Murphy had the pleasure of working with Officer George one snowy afternoon. They were on patrol when the radio dispatcher announced a man shot near Elston near Pulaski. George activated the blue lights, Murph hit the siren and off they went. More information followed and the job sounded more bona fide the closer they got. Pushing the old Chevy to her limits, they arrived at the restaurant supply company in a matter of minutes. Exiting the squad car, they observed an elderly gentleman, dressed in an overcoat lying on the ground in the newly fallen snow. Surrounded by police officers and showing signs of trauma, with his last breath, he described the man who shot him. Their victim stated how he was robbed at a gun point by two young Latinos and after handing over the requested briefcase, they shot him in the chest. The victim succumbed to his injuries in the parking lot of the supply company that he built it into a well-respected business.

Earlier in the evening, a man came home from work and went to park in his garage only to be prevented by an automobile blocking his door. Sounding his horn, the offending vehicle pulled away only to park by his neighbor's garage, two doors down. After copying down the license plate number, the man went into his house and dialed 911 to report this individual. By the time the assigned beat car arrived, the vehicle was long gone.

Back at the scene of the robbery/shooting, officers Kenny, Kelly, and Stephen were already questioning witnesses. One of the officers was sharp enough to tie the suspicious vehicle call with the robbery, although not immediately. After the connection was made, the dispatcher researched the radio archives and retrieved the license plate number from the suspicious vehicle. The plate number was broadcast in the city-wide radio zone as being wanted for questioning in connection with the very recent robbery/homicide.

The flash message described an older, smaller, grey vehicle occupied by a Hispanic male in his twenties. The shooters were described as Hispanic males in their twenties as well. All were dressed in hoodies and dark clothing. Murphy and George drove the streets and alleys attempting to locate this vehicle when, at about 10:30 pm, a sergeant broadcast over the radio that he was pulling the wanted vehicle over. In minutes George and Murphy were on the scene removing a couple of Hispanic females from the vehicle. The driver told the sergeant that her boyfriend and two others arrived home in a state of panic. When she inquired what was wrong they mumbled that they did something bad and directed the girlfriend to return to the area around Elston and Pulaski and see what was going on. Murph determined the address of the driver's residents from running the plate number on their portable computer. George and he sped to the address in the 14th District. They requested backup from the other and within seconds had the residence surrounded. A man with an infant in his arms answered Murphy's knock on the front door. Through the front windows, Murph observed three Hispanic males run toward the rear of the apartment. Shouting on the radio, he alerted the officers in the rear of the building as their small group entered the front. With guns drawn and readied, the officers trapped the individuals into a corner of a rear bedroom. All were clad in t-shirts, dark pants, and no shoes. After securing the offenders, Murph opened the triple locked rear door and allowed officers guarding the rear to enter. A search revealed hidden hoodies stuffed in the window well, still covered with snow. The offenders denied being outside on this wintery night, but their shoes were sitting in puddles of water at the front door. Evidence was building and alibis were crumbling. Calling for transports, all three subjects were separated and taken to the district for further questioning. An evidence technician was requested for photos and to recover the clothing stuffed in the window well. After a short time, the detectives handling the case had everybody involved transferred to the Area Detective Headquarters for a more detailed investigation.

Interviews were taken and interrogations were used to get two arrestees to formally state that they were the subjects who robbed and murdered the owner of the restaurant supply company. One arrestee explained that he made a delivery to the supply house months earlier and observed the victim with what he considered a large amount of cash. This vision resurfaced as he was discussing bills with his girlfriend. He told her he knew where to get some quick cash and the robbery scheme was hatched. Recruiting another gang member, they placed the business under surveillance night after night. The hoodlums would hunker down in a doorway across the street from the victim's office while smoking a joint and drinking forty-ounce beers. They memorized his every move.

Choosing a snowy night, they borrowed the girlfriend's car and drove to the scene, stopping only to pick up a third member. Two of the robbers secreted themselves again across from the target, while the get-away driver waited in a nearby alley. When the lights of the office dimmed, they set in motion a life-altering plan. The target walked out into the falling snow after locking the front door for the last time. The sequestered robbers, dressed in dark hoodies, approached with a small caliber gun in hand. They startled the victim. Demanding money and valuables, they took what the victim surrendered; an old leather briefcase filled with useless paperwork. Before they fled, and for no obvious reason, they shot him in the chest. Retreating to the get-away vehicle, they opened the briefcase to find receipts and other worthless business documents. Fleeing down the alley, the briefcase and contents were thrown to the wind. The gun was also pitched out the car window as the escaping vehicle and occupants separated themselves from any evidence connecting them to this event. Visibly shaken, the trio drove home and was immediately confronted by the girlfriend who guessed something terrible had occurred. She was directed to go back to the scene and see if the police were there. Once back at the scene, she was stopped by the sergeant and the investigation started.

The car was impounded and towed as evidence. The scattered papers and briefcase were recovered and inventoried. One offender was returned to the scene by the detectives and the weapon was recovered from a rear yard.

By late morning, detectives formally charged the three arrestees with the robbery and murder of the victim. Detectives also had obtained written confessions from two offenders admitting their roles, while implicating the third.

By the time the offenders were brought to trial, Murphy had been promoted to sergeant and was working the midnight shift in another district. After an excruciating weeklong trial, all three offenders were declared guilty of murder during the commission of a robbery. After a conviction, there is a sentencing hearing in order to arrive at the most appropriate sentence. This hearing will be embedded in Murphy's mind forever. The victim's daughter tearfully explained to the judge, that she would never have the pleasure of her father walking her down the aisle at her wedding, nor would be able to hold his first grandchild. Baseball games and birthdays were spoken of: None of which the victim would ever take part in.

The three gang members were given long prison terms for this senseless murder.

MISS-DIRECTING TRAFFIC

Murphy and his field training officer, Officer Ed, were assigned to the intersections of Lincoln, Fullerton, and Halsted to monitor traffic congestion. The traffic lights were not working properly. At the beginning of rush hour, Murphy's FTO decided that Murph should direct traffic at the three-way intersection while he would grab his first cup of coffee. Ed took up a position in the front window, inside a diner on the corner and observed Murph's traffic control techniques. All was going well on this hot summer afternoon until a voluptuous young lady attempted to cross Murphy's intersection on the way to the beach. Clad in a tiny, tight-fitting top exposing her 'mounds of life,' she sauntered across his intersection. Being single and immediately in love, Murphy soon had the traffic from Lincoln and Fullerton running into one another. Through the screeching tires and blaring horns, Murph looked into the diner for help only to see his partner laughing like hell while spilling coffee all over the counter. No, he did not come to his rescue

A HECK OF A SENDOFF

A very bazaar radio assignment caught the attention of all cars in the 17th District: "A barrage of shots fired in the cemetery". Five or six cars were riding and this time, the more the merrier. Upon approaching the cemetery gates, Murph and his partner heard another salvo of gunfire. Broadcasting that information on the radio, even more units started riding. The cemetery was awash in blue and white squad cars, blue lights rebounded off grave stones and markers. As they approached the single group of mourners, it was like a starter's pistol went off. People began running everywhere; across graves and through bushes. Cars began screeching tires and fleeing in all directions on those manicure trails only found in cemeteries. The scene was utter chaos.

A "twenty-one gun" salute had taken place for the recently departed. Luckily, there was only the single funeral taking place and the involved subjects were easily identified. Officers had foot chases everywhere. Guns were secreted by the funeral-goers and slowing recovered by police officers. Those involved were being chased down and handcuffed.

The only entry/exit to the cemetery was quickly blockaded with Chicago police cars. Automobiles were searched before being permitted to leave the cemetery and more weapons were confiscated. Handcuffed subjects sat in the grass next to a squad car with its trunk open for the collection and storage of seized weapons

The field lieutenant arrived on the scene and immediately ordered the car searches to be halted: the remaining twenty or so cars in the funeral procession were allowed to leave unmolested by the police. It was later learned that the priest that left took with him a small arsenal in the trunk of his car.

Numerous handguns were confiscated and half dozen men went to jail. Apparently in the old country, a twenty-one gun salute was the custom. In the United States it's frowned upon.

WAS HE ALIVE?

In 1978, Murphy was working a beat car in the Cabrini Green Housing Projects. Murphy and his partner responded to what would be the second homicide of his career. In the basement of one of the high rises, the custodian found a human foot sticking out of the garbage dumpster. There was a body, but with a twist: this fellow was in seven pieces. The evidence revealed that he had entered the garbage chute from the sixth floor and slid to his demise. This particular building had a working garbage blender that was designed to chop the garbage as it was tossed down the chute. This way it could be compacted and take up less space. The system worked so well, the deceased was in pieces with his internal organs spilled out throughout the dumpster. The detective, knowing that Murphy was new on the job, threw him a set of gloves and requested that he assist him in locating all of the victim. Once the black plastic body bag was laid out, they began their search. They pulled body parts out and placed them into the bag, like completing a three-dimensional jigsaw puzzle. At one point the detective said, "Hey, hey, hey, look what I found." Then he yanked the head out and held it up by the hair. Murphy nervously chuckled and continued digging. Again, the second detective, trying to freak him out, started singing the old kid's song, "The knee bone's connected to the leg bone, the leg bone's connected to the ankle bone..." as he was pulling body parts from the dumpster. After locating the seven main pieces and then scooping up the innards, they reassembled the human body and called for a wagon to transport it to the city morgue.

The detectives took over the investigation and Murph and his partner submitted their preliminary report listing the deceased as John Doe, cause of death unknown. The following day's newspaper had a short news story about the body of a homeless man found in the garbage dumpster. Even though the victim had green alligator shoes, probably worth two hundred dollars back in 1978, the newspapers played this to be a derelict that slept in garbage dumpsters to keep warm. They did not explain how he wound up in seven pieces. Murphy's informal explanation was that a dope deal went bad and the alligator shoe guy was thrown down the chute deliberately.

Sometimes at night, Murphy thinks about this guy. He often wonders if alligator shoe guy was alive when he was tossed down the chute. If so, did he hear the switch trigger the blades to start twirling?

A DOSE OF REALITY

Driving westbound on North Avenue, Murphy observed an expensive new car pull a U-turn at a high rate of speed. Being brand new, alone, and aggressive, he threw the blue lights on and initiated one of his first traffic stops. The driver did not have a driver's license and was placed under arrest and handcuffed. A search revealed a small bag of cocaine in his pocket and he was placed in the back of the squad car. His "girlfriend," who Murph believe was actually a high priced hooker, was asked for identification and placed under arrest when a cursory look into her purse revealed another bag of cocaine. Everybody involved was transported into the station. A closer search of the vehicle, for inventory purposes, uncovered five thousand dollars, rubber-banded together in ten dollar increments, fifty grams of marijuana, and sixty grams of cocaine in the trunk.

With the assistance of his lieutenant, six pages of inventory were completed, the car was impounded, two arrests were made, and a large quantity of narcotics was removed from the street. Now the interesting part of the story begins.

During the probable cause court appearance, an infamous defense attorney approached Murphy and offered him five hundred dollars to have amnesia. After conferring with salty veterans, Murphy realized he had little chance of winning this case so he counter-offered. Murphy told the attorney that if he took the five thousand dollars that Murph inventoried and donated it to the Gold Star families, families of police officers killed in the line of duty, Murphy would suffer a memory loss. The attorney replied that he would get back to him.

Not hearing from him, Murphy arrived in narcotics court for the trial and the case was immediately called in front of the judge. Instantly, he dismissed the charges against the female siting a lack of probable cause to look into her purse. He then ignored the probable cause on the arrest of the male and dismissed the charges against him. The judge began lecturing Murphy about the rules of inventorying a vehicle, stating that Murphy needed to inventory all items of value found in the vehicle and not cherry-pick items to inventory, such as the narcotics and cash. Murphy waved six full pages of inventories and attempted to explain that more than forty-five items were inventoried exactly according to the rules of evidence and under the direct supervision of his Field Lieutenant. Murphy was warned by the State's Attorney to remain quiet and not get the judge angry. All charges were dismissed and the defendant regained control of his five thousand dollars. Murphy wondered in a loud voice, "Who got paid off?" as he angrily exited the court room.

Years went by and Murphy refused to make arrests for narcotics. Finally, the Federal Bureau of Investigation initiated Operation Grey Lord, an undercover sting, investigating corruption in the Cook County Court Systems. The attorney involved in his case was indicted as well as the judge. Both pleaded guilty and were respectively sentenced to two years and six years in the Federal Penitentiary. It was explained later to this uneducated rookie that the attorney probably had passed a thousand dollars to the judge and pocketed the remaining four thousand dollars from the money Murphy inventoried. His faith was somewhat restored in the system. But, narcotics were never a strong suit of his police career. If a person needed to be arrested for possession, Murph called a tactical team and the arrest was turned over to them.

WHERE THE HELL'S THE RECRUIT?

In October 1995, Murphy was working in the 17th District as an FTO, field training officer. His partner was a brand-spanking new recruit by the name of Denny, spit-shined and all. Their very first job was a burglary report. This was good because it would hone the recruit's report writing skill, the most overlooked skill in police work. Murphy was standing on a third floor back porch enjoying the view while Denny occupied his time with the victim. The radio burst with a dispatch of a pursuit. The district's evidence technician, Louie, was chasing a motorcycle south on Kedzie with two known gang members fleeing. The passenger was wanted for a shooting that recently occurred across the border in the 14th District. Realizing that the chase was coming toward their location and guessing that the recruit would rather get involved in some real police work, Murph grabbed him. He shouted to the burglary victim that they would return to complete the report. Was Murphy ever wrong!

Bounding down the stairs, they jumped into the squad car and Murphy floored it. The old Chevy took off westbound down Belmont, in the direction of the vehicle pursuit. Moments before reaching Kedzie, the motorcycle turned directly in front of them. They were now the primary pursuit car. Flying down Belmont, a few feet behind the wanted subjects, Denny was expertly shouting directions on the radio. He was now the lifeline between them and any help that they may need. The motorcycle swerved in and out of traffic and they stayed on their tail like flies on crap. Crossing the border into the 14th District they flew, taking side streets and at one point forcing the motorcycle up on the sidewalk. Now running parallel to the bike, the motorcycle passenger drew a pistol and fired a round missing them. Immediately afterward they hit a bump in the sidewalk and the pistol jumped from his hand. Murphy told Denny "We're going to end this thing." At the end of the block, Murphy pulled the squad car around the corner and blocked their path into the crosswalk. He knew if they made the street they could out run them. The motorcycle driver expertly slammed on the breaks, slid around the turn and continued down the sidewalk. Shouting to Denny to hold on, Murph's squad jumped the curb, tearing up the lawn and sliding across the sidewalk blocking the motorcycle's path. Like the sound of a bomb going off, the bike struck the side of the squad car. Murphy jumped out with pistol in hand and a local hoodlum nicknamed Widow-Maker, rolled to a stop, regained his bearings, and took off southbound. The driver lay on the ground with Murph's pistol aimed at the head. He was waiting for his partner to assist him, but he stayed seated in the car. Murphy was shouting at the driver to stay down or he'd shoot him, while screaming at his partner to get his fuckin ass out there and help him. Moments later, Denny dove out the passenger side window and landed on the motorcycle. He took control of the prone arrestee and Murphy started his foot pursuit of Widow-Maker. Being out of their district on a Sunday, Murphy was concerned about the response time for assistance. But within seconds of shouting for help on the radio, he could hear the sirens of the 14th District cars flying in to assist them. Down the alleys, through yards, over fences, Murphy gave a final address of somewhere on Christiana Street. After seven blocks of running and jumping, Murph had finally lost sight of Widow-Maker and couldn't go any further, he was completely exhausted. A few seconds later, a 14th District car shouted that they had him trapped in some bushes. After cell lights and night sticks were used to subdue him, Widow-Maker was placed under arrest and transported into the 17th District for charging. Another wagon swung by and picked up the prisoner that the recruit was guarding. A .40 caliber, semi-automatic Ruger with ten live rounds was recovered from the sidewalk. One spent shell casing was also taken into evidence.

Widow-Maker was charged with aggravated battery to a police officer, aggravated assault of two police officers, unlawful use of a weapon by a felon, discharge of a firearm, and the original aggravated battery charges for shooting a rival gang member a couple of nights earlier. He went to Cook County Jail. The motorcycle driver was charged with reckless conduct and aggravated assault, and assorted traffic offenses. He posted bond and was released later that night.

A few weeks later while Widow-Maker was resting in the county jail, waiting his day in court, the motorcycle driver was allegedly involved in a double homicide, and the wounding of a third person. It appeared that their gang had a falling out with a few of their own members. In the assassination, two carloads of gang members blocked the target car in behind an alley, where occupants from both cars exited, and began pumping bullets into the blocked in vehicle. Two persons died on the scene and the third, shot six times refused to cooperate in the investigation. The motorcycle driver fled to his home town in Mexico, and Widow-Maker was eventually sentenced to fourteen years in the penitentiary for the earlier shooting.

Now back to Denny. The impact of the motorcycle striking the squad car jammed Denny's car door, preventing it from opening. Murphy thought he froze and was ignoring his calls for assistance. Not even close. Denny was frantically pushing, shoulder slamming, and kicking at the door to get out. He eventually launched himself out the window like a rocket and crash landed on the overheated motorcycle engine, burning both hands. Not knowing where they were, and realizing that assisting units may take a while, Denny subdued the prone driver, rolled him over and handcuffed him before friendly faces showed up. Burned hands, his first car chase, and shots fired: one a hell of a day for a rookie.

HOW TO MAKE A BAD SITUATION WORSE

In the early 1990's, morale was at its lowest level in the history of the Chicago Police Department. A decision was made to raise morale. This was to be accomplished by sending a deputy from headquarters to speak to the troops in the field and discuss their concerns. After the officers were ushered into an auditorium, the deputy stood proudly in his impressive uniform. He spoke briefly about the duties and responsibilities of being a Chicago police officer then opened the floor to questions. A veteran officer asked him what he was willing to do about the poor morale among the rank and file. He replied, "If you don't like the job, quit." As you could guess, this put a damper on the Q and A session. The meeting was over.

Years later, another meeting between the street officers and the deputy grew from disagreements between the officers and the dispatchers. A dispatcher is a lifeline between the police officer on the street and his fellow officers. They can keep you safe or place you in harm's way. Generally, the dispatchers were fantastic, but Murphy and his fellow officers were going through a rough period when a certain dispatcher was not passing on all the available information about an assigned job to the responding officers. Some information was innocuous, some was outright life threatening. Beat officers were dispatched to disturbance calls and sometimes they were not being informed about weapons being present. Officers were walking into very dangerous situations involving guns and knives without any warning from the dispatchers. Shit hit the fan and street officers were screaming. A deputy was sent from the Ivy Tower to speak to the troops. During the Q and A session, Murphy asked if the dispatchers could be apprised of their dissatisfaction and would they be instructed to pass along all available information on the jobs that they dispatch. The deputy stated that he already spent a day observing the dispatchers and was very pleased with the way they handled themselves. He said flat out that the problems involved originate from the street officers and not the dispatchers. The meeting was over.

CAN'T GET UP AND WALK AWAY

Murphy acknowledged a dispatcher's request that he see a complainant about a missing six-month-old baby. This call piqued his curiosity. Murphy was directed to DCFS, Department of Children and Family Services. After arriving and explaining his presence, a secretary escorted him to a small office and introduced him to the caller. A young Hispanic woman who spoke broken English invited to Murphy sit, and motioned toward an old wooden chair. She explained that the missing six-month-old infant was a ward of the State. She was the case worker and therefore, the legal guardian. The infant was removed from the mother after birth when the child was born with a cocaine addiction. Since the birth, the child was weaned off drugs and was sent to stay with the paternal grandmother. The grandmother sought and received permission to take the child out of state and visit relatives in Mississippi. The grandmother returned on the correct date, but the child did not. The grandmother left the child with another relative in Mississippi and returned to Chicago without alerting DCFS. Murphy was called because the case worker needed a missing person's report to keep her out of trouble. She was ultimately responsible for this infant.

As he sat there listening intently, the case worker was seemingly distracted and their conversation was almost irritating her. Murphy asked the necessary questions that a sensitive investigation like this required, and she answered almost begrudgingly. She seemed annoyed when Murphy asked her how long the baby was missing. She was bothered when he inquired as to what steps she took in locating the baby. And finally she was exasperated when a Murphy asked why she didn't do more to locate the baby that she was legally responsible for.

Her entire investigation and attempt to locate this child included calling the grandmother twice on the phone and knocking on the door once at her only visit to the grandmother's apartment. Murphy sat back in the uncomfortable chair and stared at her in disbelief. He suggested that she contact her immediate supervisor and request that he meet them in her office. When asked why, Murphy explained that she was going to be place under arrest for child neglect and she would be transported into the district for processing. Murph had just gained her full attention. Her supervisor was summoned and Murphy explained that he was going to arrest the case worker for placing the infant in jeopardy. Her actions fell dramatically short of the duty and responsibility of a caseworker charged with the obligation of caring for an infant under her control.

As you could imagine, Murphy's sergeant was summoned immediately. Murphy explained the situation to him and he directed Murphy to simply write the report and not make any arrests. Murph was livid, but he did what was ordered. His report consisted of three pages of narrative. A normal report is one page, very rarely two pages. This report was three full pages describing the criminal negligence involved over a sixty day period.

A six-month-old baby simply does not get up and walk away. Murphy called the area youth office to report the missing person. In Chicago, the youth office doubles for the missing persons department. The youth officer he spoke to understood his anger and disappointment. She took the usual information and asked him to fax over a copy of the report to her office. Murphy also sent her a copy of the report through the police mail to ensure the proper follow up investigation. That Thursday afternoon, Murphy went home completely frustrated. He was off work until Monday, which meant he had a three-day weekend to simmer about the baby that "got up and walked away."

That Sunday morning, Murphy kicked back in his recliner to read the local newspaper. On the front page was the question, *How can DCFS lose an infant?* Murph was blown away. He showed his wife the article and the narrative was almost verbatim of his missing person's report. Murphy didn't know what to make of the article. He was overjoyed that somebody was actually paying the proper attention to such a grievous error in judgement involving an infant. An investigation into DCFS was immediately initiated and when he was back at work on Monday, he contacted the youth officer he originally spoke to. Murphy asked if she knew anything about the newspaper report. She said that she had a friend at the newspaper and seeing that Murphy was so troubled, she thought she would do something about it. She supplied the newspaper with enough information to stoke their curiosity and they initiated their own investigation. The report instituted sweeping changes in protocol at the child service agency and Murphy felt vindicated in his original decision to arrest the case worker. Murphy thanked the youth officer and his faith in the police department was restored.

FILL-INS FOR HIRE

A description of an offender wanted for a major theft was broadcast in the 17th District. Murphy and his partner, John, started their shift at about 4:30 pm and just heard the ending. They started their shift driving Lawrence Avenue keeping an eye out for the male Korean thief. After about an hour, their persistence paid dividends, they spotted a possible subject. A traffic stop was made and the individual was patted down for weapons. The search revealed a very large amount of currency in his possession. After failing to adequately satisfy their curiosity, the subject was taken into the district for investigation.

Detectives were fairly certain that this was the individual who had stolen a very large amount of money from a Korean store owner, but they would need more proof. A lineup was requested and they needed three more Korean males as fill for the lineup to be permissible. After calling other districts to no avail, Murphy had an idea. He and John went back to Lawrence Ave, going from restaurant to restaurant; they found three subjects willing to donate thirty minutes of their time to help the police. Albeit, for dinner money.

The line-up was held and the subject was identified by the owner as the man who stole over five thousand dollars from him. He was charged with felony theft and Murph and John drove their fill-ins back to their dinner engagements. A few dollars was passed to their new friends and Murphy and John developed a new resource for lineup stand-ins.

OBSERVING THE POLICE IN ACTION

While still in the Chicago Police Academy, Murphy was supposedly studying for an exam. Gazing out the second floor window he observed two men breaking into the park district building across the street. Before he could say anything, a wild herd of recruits about thirty strong was charging toward the crooks. The burglars looked up from their handy work and saw a mass of blue charging them. Outnumbered fifteen to one, the burglars quickly surrendered after a short foot chase. Yes. They are that stupid. Breaking into a building, across from the police academy, during daylight hours, while about two hundred recruits are there training, is a pretty stupid thing to do.

DOG NEARLY GAVE ME A HEART ATTACK

Being a dog lover, Murphy was driving past the park when a man was walking his miniature companion. A mixed breed of unknown source, the pooch looked friendly. Waiting to cross the street, master and dog stood at attention. Murph pulled the squad close by and the dog reacted. After taking two rapid steps toward the squad car, the dog sprung through the window and landed cleanly in Murphy's lap. The fifteen-pound rocket just stared into Murphy's eyes requesting a rub.

The owner quickly apologized, Murphy thought his heart stopped, and the little pooch just made himself comfortable. Realizing the harmlessness, Murph petted the pooch and scratched behind his ears. A friend was made for life. The pooch was retrieved and Murphy's heart rate eventually returned to normal.

THE KID'S LAST DAY

Out of roll call Murphy's squad car was acting up so he thought he would drive it to the area for a check-up. Pulling up to Addison and California, Murphy observed a commotion in the street by a school. A forty-foot tractor trailer was halfway around the turn and decided to stop in the intersection. Upon closer review, the driver was too occupied with something around the rear tire to even see Murphy's blue lights. Immediately Murphy recognized the problem; a bicycle was sticking out from the double axel. Upon closer review, Murphy's heart sank into his stomach. Two legs and arms were visible along with a torso, minus the head. The young boy had tried to beat the tractor trailer around the turn and lost. He skidded under the rear wheels and was instantly crushed. This occurred so quickly there was no time to suffer.

Another beat car was already assigned the job and Murphy stuck around to assist. An ambulance crew was on scene in minutes and placed the remains in a bag for transport to the morgue. The lone fire truck washed down the street and within an hour traffic was moving like normal. People driving by had no idea that a young man had lost his life just minutes before.

CHANGE OF HEART

People always hear about police discretion, but do they really understand the concept. While patrolling the 17ᵗʰ District, Murphy and his old buddy officer Pete observed a person driving recklessly. During the traffic stop, Murphy located five cans of beer stuffed under the driver's seat, still connected by the plastic rings. Questioning the underage driver about the beer, he responded with a belligerent attitude declaring that he was simply a few months short of the required drinking age. The officers explained that with or without the proper age requirement he could not drive a car around while drinking. It was in violation of the law to possess any open liquor in an automobile in the state of Illinois. His attitude eventually got the best of them, and he got himself arrested. In the ten-minute ride to the station, he became remorseful and genuinely regretful for the earlier attitude issues. With the new attitude, Pete and Murph, believing that the lesson was learned, decided to reduce the charges to disorderly conduct and allow him to skate on the alcohol charge. They explained their change of mind, and with that decision, they drove into the nearest alley and threw the beer into a garbage dumpster.

But as we all know, no good deed goes unpunished. Once they entered the district station, the prisoner once again started with the verbal attacks. He was going to get Pete and Murph fired. Irritated because they had already disposed of the evidence, Murphy asked Pete to start writing the arrest report as he had something that required his immediate attention. Murphy took the squad car and drove back to where they disposed of the beer. After rummaging through the dumpster he found the discarded five cans of beer. Murphy returned to the station and inventoried the beer as evidence and then charged their belligerent friend with open alcohol in a vehicle. Murphy truly believed justice comes in many forms.

CHECK OUT THAT TEENAGE CUTIE

Officers Tom and Murphy were bored and getting more bored by the minute. Driving around people watching Tom spotted a pleasing figure meandering down the block. A young girl was treating them to a runway-style walk. Tom was ogling and smiling but as they approached, Tom turned sour. He shouted, "Ah shit!" Murph asked what was wrong. Tom, with head hung and face drooping explained that his daughter was about that same age. And if they were ogling this young girl, other coppers were probably doing the same to his daughter.

THE HYPOCRISY

Murphy and his regular partner Dirk were instructed to meet with a priest at his rectory. It was a warm summer morning and they arrived ten minutes before the meeting time. They checked in with the secretary and were escorted to a sitting area. After about twenty-five minutes, they were becoming very anxious. The priest finally arrived, dressed in a pair of jogging shorts and top, with a towel wrapped around his neck. Apparently his jog was more important than being on time for a meeting that he requested with two on-duty police officers.

He quickly relayed his demands that they spend more time patrolling around his school and church grounds, looking for suspicious people. With no description and now being very annoyed, Dirk and Murphy left their meeting.

That Sunday, Dirk and Murph patrolled the area around the church. As they sat on the corner and people watched, they observed a young mother struggling to push a baby buggy down the curb and into the street. She then continued down the street from one end of the block to the other and struggled again to pull the buggy back onto the sidewalk. After realizing why, Dirk and Murphy glanced at each other. Cars were parked illegally on every part of the street, sidewalk and everywhere else you could fit an automobile. The sidewalk in front of the church was about thirty feet wide and another thirty feet from the actual doors to the curb, all jammed with parked cars. After running license plates, they found out that the car parked on the sidewalk up against the church wall, was the priest's car. Dirk and Murph were thoroughly disgusted. They pulled out their dusty ticket books and started writing parking tickets on the cars parked on the sidewalk, those in the crosswalks and others parked on fire hydrants. They placed the last ticket on the windshield when the church doors sprung open. Out came the rejuvenated Christians as Dirk and Murphy made a quick escape. Driving directly to the station, they marched into the watch commander's office and plopped down seventeen parking citations on his desk. The lieutenant quizzically looked up and asked, "What are these?" They responded that he would find out very quickly. Dirk and Murphy started backing out of the office as the desk crew started yelling, "watch commander on line one, watch commander on line two...." The lieutenant's phone bank was lighting up like a Christmas tree.

After taking a few calls the lieutenant called them back in and requested an explanation. They explained about the deliberate tardiness and the cavalier attitude the priest took during his meeting. They explained the young mother being forced to push her baby into the street because of all the cars blocking the sidewalks and crosswalks. The lieutenant thanked them and sent them back on patrol.

All the parking citations were put through the proper channels and none were quashed. The priest never requested another meeting with Dirk and Murphy again.

WHAT A WAY TO GO

The radio call explained a man walking his dog found what appeared to be a human body. Murphy activated the Mars lights, hit the siren and steered the squad car towards Gompers Park. Up and over the curb he drove, very carefully so as not the get the car stuck in the soft mud that the latest rain produced. Following the chain linked fence to a tree with a large overhanging branch, they spotted a familiar looking object lying under the tree. His partner lit it up with the spotlight: Yep, they had a body. Stepping out of the car gingerly, so as not to destroy any possible evidence, they checked on the state of their victim. It was very apparent that he was dead. Murphy made the proper notifications as his partner cordoned off the area with red tape. Their supervisor was notified, as well as the detectives and the watch commander. The paramedics arrive on scene, but their job was simply to pronounce the subject deceased.

After the detectives arrived they move in for a closer look. It was an apparent suicide, the way the body was originally leaned up against the tree. Alongside him was an open pack of cigarettes and a half-pint of whiskey. Perched in his lap was a sawed off shotgun. This individual clearly planned on taking his own life and chose this remote spot in the park to do so.

Reconstructing the crime scene, they concluded that he leaned against the tree, finished what was to be his final cigarette while sipping from the bottle of whiskey. He then placed the shotgun into his mouth and pulled the trigger. Apparently and unintentionally, at the very last moment he turned his face to the side, causing the blast from the shot gun to miss killing him instantly but instead causing him to bleed to death. What a nasty, lonely way to go.

Murphy always considered suicide to be a very personal choice, but he have often wondered how long this man lived before succumbing to his wounds.

OH BOY!

Monday morning was busier than normal in the district. Most calls were unfounded, but you always have to assume a call is authentic when you respond, particularly burglaries and alarms. Murphy was bouncing from job to job: burglar alarms and robbery alarms, usually due to mistakes people made when opening up businesses before shutting off the alarm systems. Some calls were leftovers from the previous night, men down (drunks) and open doors, etc. Holding in the morning coffee became a very real focus of Murph's. Every time he returned from a job, the dispatcher instantly gave him another seemingly important task. Eventually something had to give. Murphy raced behind some factories that were not yet opened. At the furthest distance from any other human being, he started to relieve himself alongside the earthen berm supporting the train tracks. In the middle of his heavenly release, a commuter train rushed by. Being in the middle of such an important event, Murphy did what most people would do, he smiled. He was hoping that most early morning riders were preoccupied reading the paper, but he knows he probably amused a few. When nature calls....

HOW NOT TO MEET YOUR NEW WATCH COMMANDER

Officers Dirk and Murphy were dispatched to a local grocery store to investigate a shoplifting event. Upon arrival, they had the displeasure of meeting a screaming offender. They quickly removed him and placed the ranting and raving arrestee into their squad car. Dirk and Murph proceeded to the district to complete the arrest procedure. Following police protocol, they handcuffed one arm to the ring in the interrogation room and then Murphy went to the front desk to run a name check over the phone. He returned just in time to observe their arrestee with his pants around his ankles urinating on the floor of the police station while howling at the moon. Then it registered. Murphy remembered this subject from years earlier, following the same routine. Rules state that if the person being arrested for a minor issue like theft is determined by the arresting officers and the watch commander to be in need of mental health care, he is released without charging and is transferred to a mental health facility for evaluation. After about three hours of evaluation, if he is found sane he is then released. Murphy had this guy years ago and he did exactly that. He feigned being crazy. Murphy informed his partner and declared that he had a solution. Murph went to his personal car parked across from the station and returned with a roll of duct tape. Using a second set of handcuffs, officer Dirk and Murphy cuffed his other arm to the wall behind his back, now both hands/arms were cuffed behind him to the ring embedded in the wall. Unwilling to zip up his piss soaked pants; they pulled them up and went around his waist a couple of times with the fresh roll of grey duct tape. Needing some peace and quiet to complete their paperwork, they wrapped his head with duct tape stifling the irritating sounds flowing from his pie-hole. Murphy returned to completing the name check and Dirk went back to working on the arrest report. They were surprised by their new sergeant checking on their progress. Standing at the front desk finishing a phone conversation with LEADs, the people who do the name checks, Murphy stood by helplessly as the new sergeant opened the door to the interrogation room, glanced in and immediately slammed it shut, then made a beeline for the watch commander's office. To make things more interesting, the district had just gotten a new watch commander and Dirk and Murphy have not had the pleasure of introducing themselves. Well, that time seemed to have arrived.

Murphy tossed the phone on the desk and slid in front of the door with outstretched arms just as the watch commander walked up. Murph explained that they had a minor issue but they had it completely under control. The watch commander demanded to enter, pushing Murphy aside he viewed Dirk sitting calmly completing the paperwork while their prisoner was attached the wall slightly bending forward. He was standing in a puddle of urine, with his pissed soaked pants being held up by three layers of grey duct tape. His screams were being muffled by the two-inch-wide strips of tape wrapped unceremoniously around his head. The prisoner was on display. The captain slammed the door shut and bellowed "Whose idea was this?" Believing the captain was going to get his pound of flesh, Murphy responded that he was the culprit. The captain reached out and shook my hand and said "Good work officer, carry on." That was how Dirk and Murphy met their new watch commander.

ON THE HUNT

At about 10:00 pm, officers Ron and Murphy would start their "beer hunt" in Horner Park nestled between the Chicago River and California Avenue. Locating underage drinkers, they would confiscate their beer and after checkoff at 11:00 pm, they would have a trunk of free, cold beer. One warm sticky night, they were driving slowly along the fence dividing the park and the river when they saw a commotion alongside the river bank. On their side of the river were about ten gang members drinking their beer while shouting and swearing at an unknown group across the river. Unable to get at these gang members because of a fence, Ron and Murphy drove through the park to the street and across the bridge. East of the river they started hunting for the other group. About a hundred yards down the street, they observed a large disturbance and sped to the scene. Seeing about twenty kids, six to ten years old, they were beyond baffled. Using the spotlight they detected unknown objects in the kids' hands. Shouting instructions over the PA system, Ron and Murph began herding them into a single location, paying close attention to their hands. The officers exited their squad car ordering the subjects to drop whatever they were hiding in their little fists. As if on cue, dozens of eggs fell to the ground. Ron and Murph looked at each other smothering the laughter inside them. These little kids were throwing raw eggs at the gang bangers drinking beer across the river. Murph determined that the junior offenders were from a family party and were up to typical mischief kids their ages get into. They issued a firm warning for them to be careful of these gang members and then left them to their work. They seemed to have the situation well in hand.

THIS IS THE OPERATOR

Standing with officer Ron in front of the police station's desk, Murphy was observing an arrestee bonding out. He signed his bond slip at the desk and now stepped aside in order examines the plastic baggy containing his returned possessions. While putting his belt through his pants loops, he placed a phone call from the pay phone adjacent to the desk. Murphy assumed he was calling someone to pick him up. Ron walked behind him and with a quick peek over his shoulder, noted the phone number of the pay phone. Ron shuffled the few steps around the corner into the interrogation room and directed Murphy to let him know when the arrestee was off the phone. Following instructions, without any inkling of what Ron was doing, Murphy gave the hi sign the moment the pay phone was hung up. Ron immediately called the pay phone and the user, who was walking away, made a one-hundred and eighty degree turn and answered the phone he had just hung up. Murphy heard Ron explain into the phone that he was the operator and that the caller had to deposit fifty cents more. This fellow, still in a drunken stupor, who just spent the night sleeping in a cold cell, secured two quarters and deposited them into the pay phone. He hung up without any further words being exchanged and promptly made his way out the front doors. Now being totally confused, Murph stood watching Ron. In a flash, Ron hung up his phone, jumped from his seat and walked to the pay phone and retrieved the two quarters from the coin return and said to Murph, "Ok, I'm finished, let's go." Even after they entered their squad car, Murphy just stared at Ron in amusement.

GREAT CAR CHASE/CRASHES

One of the best car chase/crashes Murphy had ever been part of took place in 1978. Working midnights, he just pulled out of the old 18th District station on Chicago Avenue. Someone on the radio screamed that they were chasing a vehicle on La Salle Street. Murphy was sitting at the intersection at Chicago at La Salle. It was very early morning and the traffic was almost non-existent. An escaped mental patient from a nearby mental health facility had jumped into a vehicle and was now leading a half dozen police cars on a chase. Murphy pulled his squad into the middle of the intersection and looked south to see a short line of blue lights trailing a vehicle coming directly at him. He waited until they were fast approaching and when the lead vehicle got within fifty yards of the intersection, Murphy promptly turned on his blue lights, and then quickly backed out of the intersection. The fleeing vehicle attempted to veer around his squad, over-corrected and lost control. The escape psychiatric patient flew up the sidewalk which sent him airborne through the Moody Bible Institute's front window. After plowing down a dozen shelves, the vehicle came to a halt in the rear of the building. With police cars screeching to the curb, radios blearing, flying debris and falling glass,theoffender nonchalantly walked out through the front store window and straight to a waiting squad car. Returned to the hospital he initially fled from, he was examined in the emergency room and determined to be in fine health. In the matter of a few short hours, he was back in his original hospital room sleeping like a baby and all the police officers were back on routine patrol. The winner that night was the board-up service.

TESTING THE NEW PEPPER SPRAY

Early one morning, a call of a "downer" was dispatched to a fellow officer. He happened to be the same officer who just bought pepper spray for the first time, and was very curious about its effectiveness. After he arrived on the scene to find a one-legged, homeless drunk, lying on the sidewalk with his private parts hanging out, he requested a wagon to transport him to a shelter. The downer was blocking the CTA bus passengers from getting on or off the bus. To add difficulty, he had urinated on the sidewalk while lying on his side and the trail of urine flowed down to the curb. This accomplishment was completed in front of about fifteen bus riders.

The dispatcher notified the officer that no wagons were available in the district. The officer requested any wagon from an adjacent district. None were available. The dispatcher asked if a Chicago Fire Department Ambulance should be dispatched. The officer replied he did not want to tie up an ambulance on a "regular" piss bum. Murphy was listening to the conversation intently, he knew what was coming. The officer stated he was going to "Try something." Seconds later, he informed the dispatcher that the inebriate was hobbling down the street on one leg.

While listening intently, Murphy visualized the officer trying everything in his power to stand this well-known drunk up. After going through the list of requests Murph can only guess that the officer leaned over the urine soaked, one legged bum, and directed a blast of pepper spray into his nose. This caused the one-legged drunk to instantly jump to his one foot and start to hobble down Belmont Avenue with the assistance of his crutch.

POLICE TICKET SLOW-DOWN

Everybody's heard of the blue flu. This is when police officers are in the midst of a contract dispute and some call in sick to force the city's hand at the bargaining table. Another tactic was a ticket slowdown. This is when officers cease writing tickets. This hurts the city in the pocketbook. They were doing exactly that when their watch commander came to roll call and made a succinct, but very effective speech. He stated, with a foreboding tone, that he would be inspecting citation books the following work day, and those officers who have not written a ticket should be prepared to find another place to work. The captain was an excellent boss to work for as long as you "towed the line." Once you crossed him, your police life was over. The following day citation books were indeed inspected and all officers passed.

HE DESERVED IT

Every district has its share of street people. They all have an assortment of living arrangements; some sleep under bridges, others under viaducts. Some sleep in shelters and wander the streets during the daylight hours begging for handouts or change. Still others drink and do drugs to excess, then bother the hell out of good decent people. The following story is about that single, annoying drunk that simply won't leave you alone.

Officers Ron and Murphy were assigned a call of a disturbance with an inebriated subject, who was verbally assaulting people walking past him on the sidewalk. As soon as the officers arrived on the scene, they recognized him as a regular customer. He averaged an arrest per week. As Ron and Murphy approached him, he began to get belligerent and aggressive. They quickly handcuffed him, preventing him from forcing a violent confrontation. He was still hootin and hollering, wanting to kick their asses. Shouting they don't have the right to arrest him and that he has constitutional rights to talk to people on the street. After Ron and Murph arrived at the police station, they were in the interrogation room completing reports when he started up again, driving them crazy. Ron told Murphy that he had an idea. He disappeared and Murphy continued with the arrest report, attempting to put the drunk into the lockup as quickly as possible.

Ron returned five minutes later with a policewoman dressed in her civilian coat covering her police uniform. Ron pointed to the prisoner and sternly asks her, "Is that the man who did it?" She replied "Yes, that's the man." She put her hands to her face as she started sobbing uncontrollably. Ron pretended to attempt to comfort her as he assisted her out of the interrogation room. All the while, the arrestee was sobering up and was now very curious about what had just taken place. A minute later Ron walked in and announced that the derelict is going to be charged with rape.

Paperwork completed, the prisoner was now escorted to the lockup where Ron explained he would wait until he was presented to a judge in the morning for the arraignment on the rape charges. Ron and Murph left the station and headed for coffee as the belligerent drunk decried his innocence. Of course he was ignored because everybody in the station understood he was only charged with simple disorderly conduct, and not rape. You don't have to beat a prisoner to get even with him.

CAPS MEETING AND CAR CHASES

Officers Dirk and Murphy planned to silence the three old farts that attended the monthly CAPS meeting religiously. They were there simply to cause a ruckus and complain about never seeing the police anywhere on the beat. At times, their antics took over the meeting so that the officers couldn't get any real service work accomplished.

If they wanted to see the police more often, Dirk and Murph would comply. While working afternoons, once a week they would obtain the assistance of another marked police car and an unmarked one as well. Starting a block away from the group leader's house, the unmarked car would speed past his house with two marked squad cars pursuing it with sirens blaring and blue lights flashing. This bit of police hijinks regularly took place on a weekly basis. Eventually they discontinued the car chases because one night during their phony chase, low and behold they picked up an extra squad car in the pursuit. Screaming 'scatter' over the radio, they all went different directions. Regrouping minutes later to try and figure out who the uninvited guest was, they observed a police car slowly approaching down the alley minus headlights. A couple of the girls pulled up munching on a bag of candy, inquiring who they were chasing. Dirk and Murphy cancelled future chases for safety sake. But, never again could these disruptive old farts say they never saw the police on their beat.

SEARCHING A BEAUTIFUL YOUNG LADY

In 1978, Murphy came off recruit probation and he was finally a 'real' police officer. He and officer Ed were working the north end of the 18th District. Late one evening they spotted a very attractive, very petite, Puerto Rican girl crossing the street. She was swaying her hips right to left, tip-toeing around the puddles, while balancing her shoes daintily in one hand. She was apparently a little tipsy so Ed and Murphy were genuinely concerned about her well-being at this late hour. They exited the squad car and called her over. Ed checked her identification while Murph stood by and ogled. Ed soon pushed her against the squad car and began to search her tiny frame, sliding his hands up and down her revealing dress. Murphy stood by in amazement, not believing what he was seeing. After a long moment, Ed called him over and told 'Nancy' to tell him her name while nodding at Murphy. With a deep tenor-like voice, she blurted out: "Tony." Murphy had been introduced to his first transvestite.

VICTIM GETS EVEN

A 911 call from a burglary victim stated he was holding an offender for the police. As Murphy pulled his squad car up to the curb, he already heard the sixteen-year-old kid screaming. The kid burglar demanded that Murphy arrest the victim for slapping him after he caught him in his garage. After a very brief investigation, Murph determined that this loud-mouthed kid broke the window of this man's garage and illegally entered it to see what he could steal. He already knew that as a juvenile, he would not face any serious discipline. But, to add salt to the wound, he demanded that Murphy arrest the home owner for interrupting his burglary and slapping him in the face. The home owner related that he heard a commotion in the garage and observed that the side window was broken. He entered and found the burglar attempting to escape and briefly struggled with him when he was forced to slap him. Nothing was taken and the broken window could easily be fixed, but he had spent over one year refurbishing a motorcycle. When the teenage perpetrator entered the garage, he knocked the bike over, scratching the unique paint job. While Murphy was listening to the victim calmly explain his thoughts, the juvenile continued to shout that he knew his rights. After evaluating the situation Murph made a decision. He told the little shithead to "shut up." He took him by the arm and threw him back into the garage. He then told the victim he had thirty seconds to talk to him and explain all the work he put into restoring the motorcycle. The owner smiled and after thirty seconds the duo came out of the garage. The burglar was silent and the victim was pleased. The burglar was processed in the district and turned over to his parents with a warning to not be seen anywhere near the garage. Murphy also lied and told to him that he gave the victim his address and as a biker Murphy understood that he would take matters into his own hands, if there was a next time.

I THOUGHT IT WAS FUNNY

Officer Ron and Murphy were working beat 1732 and stopped into the station for Ron to use the washroom. Murphy sat in the car, bored. He took Ron's ticket book and opened it to the next citation to be issued. There are five copies of the traffic citation and the yellow copy goes to the traffic violator. On the backside of the yellow copy, in very small print Murph wrote "You're a Jagoff." Then he put everything back in order. When Ron returned to the squad car, Murphy suggested that they write some tickets and make their sergeant happy. Soon afterward, they stopped a violator for going through a red light, and Ron issued him a citation. Thirty minutes later, they were summoned to the district where Ron was directed to see the watch commander. Murphy stood outside the watch commander's office listening. After getting his ass handed to him, Ron stomped out the station cursing under his breath. Murphy caught up with him and asked him what happened. When he burst out with laughter Ron knew immediately Murphy was the culprit. Boredom is what you make of it.

HOW TO COOL DOWN A PARTY

Responding to a third call of a loud teenage party, four police cars showed up. The officers knocked on the door and were met with jeers from within. It appeared to be a party where mommy and daddy were away. They observed the occupants inside laughing and making fun of the police who could not make legal entry. After a few minutes of walking around the house in minor frustration, the officers left. Rumor had it that someone took the garden hose and shoved it down the vent to the clothes dryer located in the basement, turned it on and left. Believing all the partying was contained to the first floor, Murphy wondered when the leak was discovered.

KNOW WHEN TO GET OUT OF THE WAY

With about thirty minutes left in his day shift, Murphy was driving down the side streets of the 17th District trying to stay out of trouble. He spotted a guy that he just had to talk to. This guy was six-foot-four-inches tall and about two hundred-and-fifty pounds. His clothing was tattered, his long hair messed up, and he was bleeding from corner of his mouth. Oh, and he's carrying a car jack over his shoulder; no, not a tire iron, a car jack minus the base. Murphy stopped the squad car about twenty feet from him and exited, keeping a healthy distance between them. With his right hand on his service revolver, Murphy ordered the subject to stop and drop the metal jack. He obliged. Then Murphy realized his face was beat to a pulp, with cuts above his eye and a split lip that was still bleeding. Murphy had him sit on the curb and he approached very cautiously. Murphy asked for the story and he proceeded to explain that he was at the bar when three guys came in the rear door and kicked the crap out of him. He went home to get this car jack and was going back to discuss the situation with these guys and ask them why they beat him up. He didn't sound angry or drunk, just motivated. After thinking about what he would do in the same situation, Murphy said to him, "Let me get a couple of blocks away and just don't kill anybody." He thanked Murph and Murph quickly got back in the car and raced like hell back to the station. Murphy didn't hear any calls for service around that area while he was checking off and he doesn't know the outcome. But sometimes, you just have to know when to get out of the way of true justice.

THE WILY OLD VETERAN

Murphy was just coming back from three days off and working a beat car on the north end of the 18th District with Officer Joseph. Joe was reciting a list of police officers who were injured over the past, very hot, July weekend. There was an intersection on their beat that the local gang members adopted and decided to turn the fire hydrant on. This was a common practice in the heat of the summer, but this time it was different. Usually the people opening the hydrants would watch the police close them, then come out of hiding and reopen the hydrant later. This game of hide and seek was normal. But this intersection was different; the gang members did not leave when the police responded. They openly challenged the police officers who came to close the hydrant. Fights took place and many gang members and police officers were injured over the weekend. Joe and Murphy were assigned the job of closing this, once again opened fire hydrant. Murphy was edgy as he pulled the squad car to a stop kitty-corner from the flowing river. He counted eight young men standing defiantly on the corner. Murphy exited the squad and, after a brief hesitation, Joe met him at the front of the car. Slapping his night stick in his hand, Joe shouted, "Which one of you fuck'n jagoffs opened this hydrant?" Now staring at eight pissed-off bangers, all with clenched fists and grimacing faces, Joe and Murphy began walking toward their battle to be. Murph whispered to Joe, "If we get out of this alive, I am going to kill you."

Just as they crossed the street, squad cars started sliding to the curbs, with police jumping out right and left armed with night sticks and shotguns. In seconds, they quickly had the bangers outnumbered and they surrendered without a punch being thrown. The wagon rolled up and took eight gang members to jail.

Murphy was still looking at Joe, wondering what the hell he'd missed. Joe explained that his hesitation in the car was so he could get on the radio requesting assistance with no blue lights and no sirens. This way the bangers wouldn't hear their help coming in. The danger of this corner had been the discussion topic of the past few days at roll calls, and every officer on the north side of the 18th District responded to assist Joe and Murphy. Joe thought it would be fun to not tell Murphy. Talk about your ass puckering up!

WE'RE GOING DOWN

During the entire afternoon shift in the 17th District, all units were busy assisting citizens with water-related incidents. It had rained for the past few days and was raining heavy as Murphy got to work. He too was inundated with calls of flooded basements, cars stuck in the underpasses, and people simply stranded. The calls kept coming at a rapid pace, and Murph and his partner continued the good fight. The rain finally subsided and Murph took advantage of this break in the action to race to his house and inspect for damage. Five minutes away Murph gunned the engine and was hurling down Elston Avenue when all of a sudden he spotted it. While approaching the viaduct faster than he should have been, Murph hit the brakes and gradually slid into the lake formed under the viaduct. Naturally the engine waited for the deepest portion and then coughed and sputtered until it died. Sitting in the middle of three feet of water, Murph simply apologized to his partner.

The floor was now six inches of water and pouring in like a high pressure valve. Within minutes the officers had to roll down the windows and abandon ship. They climbed out the windows and crawled onto the squad car's roof. Lucky for them, a tow truck driver was watching this with interest. Being a good soul that he was, he backed his truck into the lake and with the precision of a navy diver went under water and connected the squad car to the chains. Surfacing, and Murph though he was actually laughing under water, he trudged back to his truck. After dragging the squad out with its former occupants sharing space on the roof with the blue lights, the driver smiled and left as quickly as he arrived. A city tow truck was summoned for a squad car that stalled and simply would not start. The officers soon were back on the patrol with a replacement car.

MY GUARDIAN ANGEL

Working days in the 17th is as safe as it goes, until the unexpected happens. In October 1980, Murphy was taking a simple police report at Belmont Avenue and the river when his day turned into a police nightmare. This extreme corner of the district was far away from any protection offered by his fellow officers. Murphy was putting the finishing touches on a report of a broken window when a CTA bus pulled up. The driver explained that he had an unruly passenger who was causing a disturbance. He requested that Murphy escort this individual off of the bus. This drunken guy looked fairly harmless, so Murphy started to remove him from the bus without notifying the dispatcher of his new situation. In an instant Murphy was fighting with this derelict at the front of the bus; tangled together they both tumbled out the door and into the street. Handcuffs in one hand, Murphy attempted to cuff this fighting fool as they boxed their way over to the curb. Murphy stepped on the curb, twisted his knee and down he went. This fool now has two hands on Murphy's pistol grip and was attempting to pull his revolver out of its holster. Murphy shouted out a "10-1" into the radio and began punching with one hand while securing his pistol with the other. They were at a stalemate. Murphy couldn't do much damage to him one-handed and the drunk couldn't pull the pistol from Murph's holster.

Rolling around in the street, Murphy looked up to see a young man standing over them. This led to the most bizarre conversation Murphy ever had. This stranger asked, "Do you need any help?" Murph shouted, "Yes. I need help!" He asked with curiosity what he should do. Murph replied, "Kick him." He asked where he should kick him. As time stood still, Murphy screamed, "Kick him in the fuckin head!" At that, the guardian angel kicked the drunken fool in the head like a place kicker kicking a forty-yard field goal. After three good kicks, Murphy managed to roll the angry drunk over and handcuffed him. With sirens blaring and squad cars screeching to a halt, his backup arrived. Murphy caught his wind and looked to thank this stranger, but he was nowhere to be seen.

Murphy doesn't know what would have happened if this young man had not intervened. He could only assume that the situation could have turned much worse. That incident occurred more than thirty-five years ago and Murphy still remembers it as clearly as if it took place yesterday. "Thank you, my guardian angel."

DON'T WAKE THE GIANT

Most wagon men are experienced police officers who, for their own reasons, don't enjoy doing regular police work anymore. Most are calm and quiet. Just don't piss them off.

The old wagon man got on the radio and broadcast that someone had broken into the wagon while it was parked alongside the old 17th District station. His police hat and eyeglasses were missing. The desk crew heard the broadcast, and replied over the radio that a belligerent drunk just bonded out and walked past the wagon when he left the station. Hearing the description, Murphy and his partner started to roam the alleys behind the station. Within minutes, they spotted their inebriated offender walking down the alley wearing the officer's police hat. Murphy put this information out on the radio, and immediately the wagon was pulling into the alley. Murphy stood by holding the arm of the hat thief as the wagon got closer. The wagon lurched to a stop. The driver's door flew open, and walking with a concentrated effort was a very large and angry wagon man. Murph stepped aside and the offender pushed away. With one kick to the groin, the offender was lifted off the ground about six inches. Instantly upon landing, he was mashed in the face with a hammer-like fist. Not a word was said. The hat thief was on the way back to the cell he occupied earlier. Don't piss wagon men off.

I GOT MINE, GO GET YOURS

Winter in the 17th District was kind of slow at times. Working a beat car, officers Dirk and Murphy were driving the side streets looking for any suspicious people to stop. Being close to Christmas, they were hoping to grab a burglar. Just North of Irving Park Road there were a lot of break-ins, so Dirk and Murphy concentrated their search in that area.

As they headed down one of the many side streets visited that day. Dirk spotted two individuals standing at the mouth of an alley. They saw the squad car and immediately took off running down the alley. Murphy threw the squad toward them and the chase was on. Fish-tailing around the turn, then spinning tires down the alley, it was fairly easing to catch up to them because of the five inches of newly fallen snow. The squad car's tires glided down the deep ruts and within seconds they were positioned between the runners. Murphy swung his door open knocking down the one on his side. As he slid on his face down the alley, Murphy stopped the car and shouted to Dirk, "I got mine, go get yours!" Murphy was on top of offender number one in a flash. Dirk on the other hand was now trudging down the alley in the tire rut cursing and running, cursing and running. Eventually, he came back with offender number two.

Two drug dealers hit the slammer. But more importantly, Murphy got to screw over Dirk. What a wonderful day.

NICE DOGGIE

Officers Dave and Murphy were dispatched to see what they could do about a stray dog laying between two houses. As Murphy pulled the squad car to the curb, they observed a German Shepherd shading himself on this brutally hot summer day. They didn't notice anything out of the ordinary. The dog seemed calm and was just shading himself from the hot sun. Dave and Murphy being dog lovers decided to get the dog some water. Dave filled a bowl that was supplied by a neighbor and they approached the mild-mannered canine. They were whistling and making those smooching noises you make when attempting to get the animal's attention. Dave and Murphy felt comfortable with the dog.

All of a sudden the dog locked eyes with Dave, stood up and started very slowly to amble toward him. Standing to Dave's left, Murphy signaled him to be cautious. This dog staring at Dave now made a very slow but deliberate beeline for him. Murph closed the gap between Dave and himself, drew his pistol and aimed it at the dogs mass. Shouting commands, while the officers slowly backed away did not faze their toothy friend. As the dog approached within ten feet, Murphy fired a round from his pistol into the grass. Nothing. He kept coming. Murphy fired a second round directly in front of the dog when he was at five feet and continued to shout, attempting to break his concentration on Dave. Moving alongside Dave, Murphy now aligned his sights at the dog's head, still shouting commands he had learned from K-9 officers. The canine now locked onto Murphy while he continued shouting that he didn't want to shoot him. Standing five feet apart with his sights trained on the dog's forehead, they had a staring match which lasted for a very, very long ten seconds. Then, just as casually as it all started, Mr. Shepherd simply turned and walked back to his original shaded resting spot between the houses. Dave and Murph were enormously relieved that they didn't have to harm someone's pet. They directed the nearby home owners to allow the dog to rest, leave the watering bowl out, and if he did not leave at sunset, recontact the police. Dave and Murph double-checked the area before getting off: Apparently their canine friend left for home after a long rest. It seems almost hypocritical, but police officers generally have more admiration for animals than for humans. Maybe animals are just nicer than the people we normally deal with.

TRAINING A PIT BULL WITH KITTENS AS BAIT

The CAPS meeting supplied information about a gang member training his Pit Bull by throwing kittens into the enclosed tennis court in the local park and letting his dog rip them apart. Being an animal lover, as well as having a very real disapproval of gang members, Murphy took up the quest of finding this thug and correcting his ways. One lucky day, Murphy observed Mr. Shithead leaving the park with his trainee on a lease. Murph deliberately positioned the squad car in the crosswalk to block his path. With the window rolled down, Murphy commanded that he make the dog sit so he could chat with him. Standing on the sidewalk while allowing his dog to stretch the leash trying to reach Murphy, he repeatedly insisted that he didn't hear Murphy. Asshole did not know that Murph had already drawn his .45 caliber semi-auto and had it pointed at the dog, just below the edge of the window. After the third request, Murphy exposed the barrel at window's height and pointed it at Asshole's dog. He slowly and very deliberate explained that his next move was to shoot the dog in the head. If he accidently shot Asshole in the groin he would claim that he was aiming at the ferocious dog that was attacking him and shot this poor man by accident. Asshole eventually saw Murph's point of view and commanded his dog to sit. Murphy then explained, in no uncertain terms, that he and his dog were persona non grata in the park and that for the safety of all involved should not be seen again. At the next CAPS meeting, Murphy declared all was good in River Park.

KEEP THE SERGEANT HAPPY

There are different styles of police officers; some specialize in gangs, guns, drugs, or traffic. Murphy and his partner Dirk enjoyed screwing with the gang members, and as a result, their traffic production suffered. Their sergeant was on their case to write some traffic citations. They didn't really care about how the front office regarded them, but for their sergeant they would comply.

At check-off one night, Dirk and Murphy turned in about twelve "movers," traffic citations written for moving violations. Their sergeant smiled a huge toothy grin and exclaimed that he was proud of them. He started to thumb through the citations and a joyous occasion quickly turned sour. All the citations were for speeding on the expressway. Chicago Police were not authorized to enforce speeding on the expressway system in Chicago. He never bothered them again.

BIG MISUNDERSTANDING

Murphy was working the day shift in the 17th District and stopped a car for running a red light. The car was full of teenagers. For safety sake, he separated the driver and brought him back to his squad car. Hesitantly, he followed Murph's instructions. Once at the squad car, Murphy directed him to place his hands on the car; he did not comply. Murphy took his hands and placed them on the car. He immediately took them off. Murphy glanced at the car full of potential trouble, and Murphy again ordered him to place his hands on the hood of the squad car. Disobeying Murphy's instructions, Murphy again put his hands on the car. The driver pushed back and as Murphy fell backward, he grabbed his arm. Regaining his balance, Murphy put his shoulder into the driver, and with a football blocking stance he drove him back onto the hood of the car. Murphy then handcuffed the subject and ordered the car occupants to remain in the vehicle. He then called for assistance. After his backup arrived, Murphy emptied out the car and began to interview the occupants. They informed him that the driver was deaf and could not hear Murphy's commands. After verifying this information, Murph uncuffed the driver and issued a citation for disobeying a red light, taking his driver's license as bond. Later that week, Murphy was requested to reply to a complaint registered against him on why he roughed up a deaf kid. Police work, at times, is difficult.

SOMETIMES YOU'RE JUST NOT IN THE MOOD

Not being in a very jovial mood, Murphy stopped a traffic violator. He requested his driver's license and explained to him that he drives so crappy that he doesn't deserve to drive. With that, Murph took his knife out and cut his license into eight pieces and handed it back to him. Murphy smiled, and said "Have a nice day." Murphy returned to his squad car and drove away.

POOR PIGEON

Working midnights in the 18th District got to be monotonous in the early morning hours. All the bad guys were either in jail or passed out. Murphy would sometimes amuse himself by driving along the lake front chasing pigeons. There is no way you can hit these flying rats with the squad car. They're just too quick. They tease you by strutting their stuff in the middle of the street until you are right on top of them, then they take off like feathery helicopters. It was a little game: police versus pigeon.

Murphy did this for a short while and quickly became bored. He drove around for the final forty-five minutes of his shift and headed in. As Murphy pulled into the police station parking lot, a few heads turned and followed him in. He exited the squad car to find a deceased pigeon lying across the light bar on the squad car. He had been driving around with dead this pigeon for forty-five minutes. Being embarrassed and dumbfounded, Murphy never chased pigeons again.

THE GIRLS WILL PROTECT ME

As a recruit, Murphy's field training officer Tom would explain things while on route to jobs. On the way to a bar fight, Tom said to follow his every move and only do what he does. Murphy explained he was ready and as they pulled to the front of the bar they could see that there was a lot of activity inside the place. When the squad car screeched to a halt, Murphy jumped out and forgot everything he was just taught and made a dash for the tavern door. Nightstick in hand and a superman's attitude, Murphy started in the front door alone. He was met by three gorgeous women who quickly grabbed his arms and marched him back out of the ruckus explaining that he was too young to get hurt. As Murphy was being escorted back out, the real police ran in and stopped the mini riot. As he was talking to his new lady friends, Tom walked by and just laughed.

MURPHY'S FIRST CAPS MEETING

Officers Dirk and Murphy were trained and authorized to conduct CAPS meetings. At the top of their game, they headed to Brands Park. Seated in front of approximately thirty people and their new sergeant, Dirk and Murph called their first CAPS meeting to order. Things went remarkably well for about five minutes, and then they hit a snag. A woman inquired about why she never saw the police patrolling her neighborhood and the stock answers were articulated. She wasn't buying it, and she continued to claim that the police favored other parts of the beat and ignored her block. During this verbal sparring, a beat representative came to their aid by saying she sees the beat car often on her block. Without thinking, Murphy blurted out that if the first woman was as nice as the second one, she too might see the police more often. As you could imagine, this boneheaded statement led to a huge argument and ended by the woman screaming at Murphy, "I'll never come to another meeting as long as I live." As she stormed toward the door. Murphy shouted back, "We don't need people like you at our meetings." Before the fist-a-cuffs started, the sergeant separated them; she and her husband left.

With the meeting adjourned, the sergeant marched out with a dejected expression while Dirk looked at Murphy with a toothy grin and said he thought the meeting went swimmingly.

As was protocol, the sergeant wrote a summary of the meeting and submitted it to their district commander. The district commander refused the report saying he could not send something like that downtown. Two days later Dirk and Murphy were back at the police academy sitting in CAPS training.

THE INSPECTOR AND THE CURRENCY EXCHANGE

On a real nasty afternoon, Murphy was assigned to a call of a man attempting to cash a bogus check at a local currency exchange. Being a horrible rainy afternoon, all the assist cars were tied up on accidents, so an Inspector (an Inspector is a Chicago police lieutenant, whose sole purpose was to ensure that police officers are conducting themselves according to the rules of the CPD) volunteered to be Murphy's backup. Murph responded to the location and found a young man with a counterfeit five thousand dollar check. This was the second counterfeit check he attempted to cash at that location in a week's time. Arresting and handcuffing this subject was applauded by his backup, the Inspector. He assisted Murphy in walking the prisoner to his car. Murph thanked him for the backup and they parted ways.

Once inside the protection of his squad car, Murphy looked into the rearview mirror at the inspector and announced on his radio that there was an Inspector in the 17th District, warning all other officers. He proceeded to drive his prisoner into the district for processing. Once Murphy secured his prisoner to the iron ring in the interrogation room, he was ordered to report to his watch commander's office. As Murphy approached his door, he could hear the inspector screaming about Murphy's insubordination and how disrespected he felt because of Murphy's alleged comments on the radio. Murphy's watch commander was rebutting this with personal information about the Inspector doing something similar when he was a patrolman. Murphy walked in and survived a harsh tongue lashing from the Inspector, but at no time could he accept responsibility for the radio comments. That would be admitting to violating the police department rules.

Murphy

About a week later, Murphy was working with a young recruit by the name of Curt, when they responded to a radio call of a burglar alarm at a large factory. It was a false alarm. The factory had recently changed owners and Murph didn't believe it was right to issue the new owner a citation for a false alarm, so he instructed Curt to code out the job and not to write a ticket. Thirty minutes later they were directed by their dispatcher to meet an inspector at the burglar alarm location. Naturally it was the same Inspector from the currency exchange and he inquired why they ignored police department general orders and failed to write a burglar alarm citation earlier. Murphy explained his logic and the Inspector corrected him and ordered them to write a citation. As his partner was issuing the burglar alarm citation, Murphy approached the Inspector's car. Standing at the driver's door and talking through the window, Murphy explained that he needed to clarify the misunderstanding the week earlier at the currency exchange. Murphy stated that he could not admit broadcasting "inspector in 17." the other night because it would be admitting to a rule violation. Believing the Inspector understood what Murphy was saying, with a smile he added, "And, I thought you were further away when I said it and you couldn't see my lips move." With that, the inspector just blew up. He yelled at Murphy as he retreated to his squad car. The recruit saw him jump into the car and asked, "So how did it go?" They eventually affixed the burglar citation on the front door of the factory and went for coffee. Some people just don't have a sense of humor.

HELPING OUR BURGLARY VICTIMS

A small mom and pop grocery store was burglarized and as Murphy was taking the report, the victim/owner was inquiring about ways to gain more from his insurance company than was actually taken. Murph went along with his new best friend and told him instead of reporting the four cartons of cigarettes that were stolen, Murph would document forty cases of cigarettes as being stolen as he suggested. He was ecstatic about the future reimbursement from the insurance company he was going to collect. But in Murphy's police report, he correctly summarized only four cartons being taken. Murphy often wondered what the response from his insurance company was when they received his erroneous insurance claim of forty cartons of cigarettes being stolen.

SHAGGING GOLF BALLS ON A SUMMER MORNING

Bill, a local jeweler and a friend, was in Horner Park one Sunday morning hitting golf balls with his seven iron. He would hit five balls, and then trudge a hundred yards to hunt those same balls that were scattered right and left. After observing this unnecessary physical exertion, Murph drove his paddy wagon and chased down a couple of Bill's errant shots. At that exact moment, the new field lieutenant drove up and inquired what Murphy was doing driving the wagon across the grass in the park. Without hesitation, he explained that he was chasing down errant golf balls because his friend Bill was running out of gas doing it himself. The new lieutenant glared at Murph and drove off. He never mentioned that incident again.

HOW NOT TO HANDLE
A SUICIDE CALL

Working with a recruit named George, Murphy responded to a call of a man threatening suicide. It was a teaching moment and Murphy was insistent upon teaching the recruit the real police way of handling this type of situation. After climbing two flights of stairs, they were ushered into a bedroom to view an inebriated young man perched on a window ledge with one leg inside and the other leg dangling outside. Not hesitating a second, Murphy exclaimed: "Either do it or don't, but quit wasting our time." The focus of their attention looked at them and with a blink of the eye disappeared out the window. Murphy immediately called an emergency on the radio and requested a fire ambulance be dispatched for a jumper. As luck would have it, he landed on rain-soaked ground and survived with just a broken arm. Murphy looked at the dazed recruit and calmly explained why not to handle a situation like that.

HOW WE MET OUR NEW SERGEANT

A new sergeant transferred into the district and was put in charge of their area of patrol. Not knowing anything about him, and not really wanting to, Murphy and his partner Dirk jumped into the squad and sped off to their beat without introducing themselves. Protocol dictated that they meet with him during the shift and properly introduce themselves in the respectful manner deserving of a man of the rank of sergeant. The night flew by. Dirk and Murphy were busy entertaining themselves by stopping the lotus cart venders, Mexican corn vendors, and confiscating their obnoxiously noisy horns. After filling a box in the trunk with confiscated horns, the long awaited radio transmission found them. The new sergeant called for a meet. They responded and drove to the destination where the sergeant was reading his paperwork with the assistance of the interior dome light. As accustomed, Murphy pulled the squad car alongside the sergeant's car, his passenger side door to the sergeant's driver's side door. Watching the sergeant finish his reading, then take the glasses off and deposit them in his front pocket, the sergeant turned toward Dirk and Murph. Murphy quickly activated the squad car's side lights, blinding the sergeant, while Dirk leaned out the window and gave the new sergeant a couple of blasts from a lotus horn. They pulled away and immediately discussed whether or not that was a good idea. After all, some sergeants don't have the sense of humor required for that type of introduction. Time would tell that this sergeant was one of those good ones.

MURDER/SUICIDE

The call "Shots fired" came out from inside an apartment. Generally, when the call is "Shots fired," it's probably not bona fide. It could be a truck backfiring, fireworks, or other noise. But, shots fired inside a building usually means trouble. Murphy's partner steered the wagon toward the address given, and within seconds they were screeching to a stop. As they ran toward the apartment complex, the outside door was already buzzing them in. Drawing their weapons, they entered and carefully made their way down the dimly lit hallway. Quietly, arriving at the apartment number given, they listened intently and heard nothing but their own hearts pounding. Counting one, two, three, they made entry. They pointed their weapons inside the door, and continued to search the small apartment cautiously. Once in the front room, Murph and his partner observed blood splatter on the walls. A woman was bleeding profusely from an apparent gunshot wound to the face. At her feet was a pistol, and a few feet from that, lay a man with an obviously fatal wound to his forehead. They continued their search, until they were certain that no one else was in the apartment. Murphy immediately called for assistance and stated they had a bona fide shooting with one dead and the other critically wounded. His partner scrounged a bathroom towel and they wrapped it around the woman's face attempting to slow the bleeding. With assist cars arriving, they wasted no time as they staggered their victim out to the wagon. Murphy climbed in the back with her and compressed the wound with the make shift bandage. His partner hit the blue lights and siren as they sped to the closest hospital. Within minutes, she was receiving the medical care required.

After the adrenaline rush subsided, the officers returned to the scene and began to piece that eerie situation together. It became apparent that the husband shot the wife in the face and put the .22 caliber pistol to his forehead, ending his own life. The bullet that struck the wife, entered one side of her cheek, and exited the other side, taking with it a good amount of her dentures. The blood splatter they originally observed, included her missing teeth, decorated the front room wall. As horrific as the wound originally looked, it was actually superficial. With the exception of the dental work, this gunshot was clean and would require a few stitches in the cheeks, but no major surgery.

The husband on the other hand was as dead as he was going to get. One .22 cal. bullet entered his forehead, and spun around the inside of his cranium, obliterating everything inside. Brain matter stained the carpet. A good guess is that he was dead before he hit the ground. The story behind the attempt murder/suicide will never be known. Tragedies like this are all too common in a big city like Chicago.

A SURPRISE FROM MY PARTNER

Making a traffic stop on a car loaded with gang members was an enjoyable event for Dirk and Murphy. They loved to spread misery on the gang members of their beat and they did it with pride. Murphy was in for a pleasant surprise. Stopping a car full of thugs was an every night event. This particular night Murphy was standing face-to-face with a shithead that believed he was the toughest person in the world. As Murphy was just getting heated up, this guy's four buddies that Dirk had been talking to walked over and proceed to kick the crap out of the Big Mouth. Murphy glance at Dirk with an astonished look, and Dirk simply nodded for him to get into the squad car. Observing this beat down and now driving away while watching Dirk smile a toothy grin, Murph finally asked what that was all about. He explained that when Murphy was woofing at Big Mouth, Dirk suggested to his four cohorts that if they did not kick his ass, they might all go to jail: Hence the beat down. Murphy congratulated Dirk for his ingenuity and back on patrol they went.

A LONELY GERMAN SOLDIER

Officers Dirk and Murphy were backing up officer Julie and her partner at a call of shouting and screaming coming from an apartment. Entering the apartment complex, Dirk heard him first. Pushing the door open, they observed a middle-aged man parading back and forth in the hallway, chanting German marching songs. As the four officers stood and observed, the German soldier marched back and forth; he was oblivious to the fact that they were there. Immediately Dirk and Murphy knew he was off his meds and this wasn't going to be easy. They looked at each other and said simultaneously, "Whenever you're ready." With a nod, Dirk sprayed the soldier in the face with pepper spray, and all four of them bum-rushed him. He was acting very strange, but he was not attempting to hurt anybody; he was just singing and marching. After a few moments of wrestling and handcuffing, they had their soldier under control. Julie and Murph escorted him down the stairs where the wagon would scoop him up for a ride to a mental evaluation. Their soldier was truly a good soldier until they reached the outer door leading to the street; this is where things got uncomfortable. He became unruly and attempted to kick and bite them. He forced them to put him on the ground. Julie and Murphy rolled him over onto his face to avoid being bitten. They took his legs and pushed them toward his upper torso avoiding the kicking feet. Apparently, they pushed too much because this caused the little soldier to expel gas. With Julie and Murphy sitting on this guy's back, lying across the sidewalk, they did not know what was making their eyes water more: the residue of pepper spray or the natural gas emitting from their prisoner. Julie and Murphy held their breath until the wagon arrived. Needless to say, they received no help from Dirk or the other officers on the scene; they were too busy laughing like hell and rooting the soldier on.

BOOM, HE'S DOWN

A great gag they liked to pull on recruits went awry. During a typical traffic stop, a salty veteran would search the vehicle, while the recruit would guard the driver standing by the squad car. In this case, Murphy pretended to search the vehicle this time, and pulled his own gun from his holster and held it up for the recruit to see. Murph shouted out, "Look what I found." Normally the recruit would simply handcuff the subject and maybe curse him a bit. Murphy's new recruit flattened this driver with a round house that Joe Fraser would be proud of all while screaming, "You dirty bastard." Murphy jumped out of the car and stopped the recruit from pummeling this guy. He picked the guy up, choking back laughter while he brushed the dirt off his shirt. Murph pulled out his handkerchief and dabbed the bloody corner of his mouth as he attempted to explain the joke that he just pulled on his new recruit. Luckily, this fellow was a sport, although not a very happy one. They parted ways with an earnest apology and Murphy and the recruit walked back to the squad car with their tails between their legs.

BE AWARE OF WHAT YOU ASK FOR

Being young and aggressive and working days in the 18th District, Murphy kept himself busy monitoring traffic. He observed an old wood-sided station wagon go through a red light and attempted to pull it over. Eventually, after trailing the vehicle for several city blocks, the driver pulled to the curb while blue lights reflected off the nearby store windows. Being irritated by his driving habits and slow response, Murphy demanded to see his driver's license. He explained he did not have one. His vehicle was piled high to the roof with miscellaneous crap. Murphy removed him from the vehicle and demanded that he show him anything in the vehicle that he thought a police officer needed to see. Murphy explained that if he had to search his car, he would empty the contents of the entire vehicle onto the street, impound it, and inventory everything. After one final warning, the driver blurted out that he had a "six-packer" stashed and Murphy ordered him to retrieve it. He opened the rear door of the vehicle and rummaged under a pile of clothes and his other worldly goods. Murphy was curious why anyone would be fearful of hiding a six pack of beer as he was easily of age. Withdrawing an item from under the pile, he turned and handed Murphy a fully loaded .38 caliber pistol. Instantly training took over and Murphy secured the weapon and quickly handcuffed the individual before he had time to realize what happened. The driver was arrested and charged accordingly. More importantly Murphy received a valuable lesson which he carried through to retirement: always be prepared for the unexpected, particularly if you request it.

LOOK, IN THE SKY

When outside agencies, such as suburban police departments or federal agencies like the FBI or DEA come into a Chicago police district, they are supposed to notify the watch commander of that district. This is normal protocol out of respect, but more importantly, if something goes wrong, the district will already have the knowledge to assist them better. The following fiasco occurred when this protocol was ignored.

Murphy and his partner just started their afternoon shift in the 17th District when a radio call was broadcast about a small air plane having difficulty, and possibly trying to land in Horner Park. Naturally a call like that attracted a lot of attention. Soon afterward, Horner Park looked like the district station at check off. Almost all of the district's patrol cars sped there and were now observing the small aircraft circling Horner Park. After numerous conversations about the situation over the police radio, they were finally ordered to return to their respective beats. It seemed that the Drug Enforcement Agency was conducting surveillance on a drug house a block west of the park. A large drug buy was about to go down, and part of their surveillance included the low flying spotter plane. They failed to notify the Chicago Police Department and as such, the surveillance was blown. Drug dealers have police scanners too.

POOR GAS STATION OWNER IN CABRINI GREEN

Once or twice a month, the police would take a report of a burglary from a kindly old gentleman that owned a broken-down gas station in the Cabrini Green Housing Projects. The items stolen were pretty much useless and without much value, but come Monday morning, he would call 911 reporting his newest break in. The old guy, determined to change this criminal habit, one day exclaimed that he was going to invest in a killer dog, a security dog. A few weeks went by and one early Monday morning, Murphy had the displeasure of being assigned a burglary at the old man's gas station. Upon arrival, he was informed that thieves had broken into his dilapidated building and they stole his killer dog. Such is life in the projects.

DON'T USE YOUR BROTHER'S NAME IN VAIN

Burning the city's gas by cruising around the 17th District, Murphy and his partner were dispatched to a "street disturbance." They located a young Hispanic man who had a terrible attitude and displayed it proudly. After he vociferously explained his constitutional rights to them, they placed him under arrest for disorderly conduct. Another upstanding citizen talked his way into being arrested. Once in the district they completed the paperwork, collected the appropriate signatures from the desk sergeant and watch commander and were on their way to the lockup with their prisoner when he revealed a secret: he was not who he said he was. For the last hour, completing the arrest report and the complaint for disorderly conduct, it seemed their friend was using his brother's name. The paperwork went through as is. You see, they didn't care. He still got locked up, albeit for a short period of time. He was released on a signature bond after signing his brother's name.

This is where the story becomes interesting. On the court date, Murphy entered the court and took his seat. He observed the defendant sitting in the rear of the room. When his brother's name was called to come before the judge, he ignored it. Murphy remembered he claimed his brother's name at the time of arrest and not his own. Murphy can only assume he was playing another game. Murph was summoned before the judge and was asked what actions he wanted to see done. Murphy requested a warrant be issued for his failing to appear in court. The judge granted his wish and the court clerk issued a bond forfeiture arrest warrant. As Murphy walked out of court, he met the defendant's gaze with a polite nod and a smile. Sitting arrogantly but clueless to what just occurred, he defiantly nodded back to Murphy as Murph left the court. Two weeks later he was re-arrested for failure to attend court, this time with no bond.

ENGLISH, I DON'T SPEAK NO ENGLISH

The voice on the radio exclaimed: "Emergency!" All was silent until the anonymous officer shouted again for help. Dirk and Murphy gazed at each other's faces hoping the other had heard a location. Intersecting streets are finally screamed through the radio. Murphy pointed the squad toward the officer's location and slammed the pedal to the floorboards. The most direct route was down a dangerously narrow side street and back out onto the main drag. The windows of the car were down, but they didn't dare place their arms outside, because they would have been taken off by a parked auto. Not being able to spare a millisecond to look down at the speedometer, Murphy had no idea of the speed they were traveling. His full concentration was on the path ten feet wide, directly in front of the squad car. Murphy considered himself an excellent driver and Dirk trusted him with his life. Murphy didn't really give a rat's ass about the car he was driving; he didn't have to pay for repairs. They were flying. Murph maneuvered by inches. All he had to do is get through another hundred feet of narrow street, but he realized that there was a blockade ahead. The car squealed to a halt and there they sat behind an empty car blocking the street. Murphy slammed on the horn and tapped the siren repeatedly, all the while shouting and cursing. After what seemed like an eternity, a squat Mexican jogged out of a nearby house and entered this vehicle. He was delivering pizzas.

A disregard (no other cars needed) was broadcast by the dispatcher; there were enough assisting units on the scene and the officer was safe. Now Murphy's focus of attention turned to the delivery man. He was now sitting in his vehicle and Murph was standing by his door screaming at the bewildered driver. Murphy shouted that he prevented them from helping a police man who was fighting for his life. Dirk was standing at the passenger's side door in case he was needed. As Dirk explained later, the veins in Murphy's neck were about to burst from his shrieking and screaming. Murphy ended his diatribe with certain exaggerated threats. These words actually shocked himself when he heard them roll off his lips. The Mexican was staring blankly into Murphy's face as Murph was going through his best imitation of a crazy man, then the driver finally broke his silence by saying, "No speak no English."

Murphy thought Dirk was going to split his pants he was laughing so hard. They retreated. Murph kept the caustic face until they made it back to the squad car, then lost it. Such an emotional roller coaster in a matter of seconds. To this day, Dirk enjoys saying 'Que'?

GREAT HUG

Working days in the 18th District and being new, Murphy was full of piss and vinegar. The call came out of a "battery-in-progress" in the exclusive east end of the 18th District. Murph activated his blue lights and was off. Being the first car on the scene, he slid to a stop and jumped out as a man and woman were in the middle of the street struggling. The woman, very petite, was putting up quite a fight against a man in his late twenties. As he approached the man, Murphy didn't give him a chance to focus his attention on him. Murph just came up rapidly and punched him as hard as he could. This seemed to work as the man went down and the woman was now free from his grasp. Murphy's eyes now fell upon the most beautiful woman he had ever seen. Dressed in a small green-and-yellow sundress with her blond hair cascading down her shoulders, she began to saunter away. Within steps, he caught up with her in the center of the intersection and placed his hands on her shoulder from behind, telling her everything was alright. She turned around and gazed into Murph's eyes and wrapped her arms tightly around his body as she pulled him in snug. This embrace lasted for what seemed like eternity. She released her grip from his waist, looked warmly into Murphy's eyes, and slapped him across the face. After taking a deep breath, he grabbed her as she slowly walked away. He gently put her arms behind her back and placed his handcuffs on her to restrain her. By now, the boyfriend had regained his composure and was explaining to Murphy that he was attempting to take her back to their apartment where she had just snorted PCP. He was simply trying to keep her safe.

Murphy placed her in the rear seat of his squad car with the intentions of taking her to the nearest hospital for emergency drug treatment. She continued to squirm around and attempted to get out of the handcuffs. Every movement she made took her tiny dress and pushed it down exposing her gorgeous breasts. Other movements tugged the soft cotton up to reveal that she had no undergarments. She could have easily competed with any of the Playboy bunnies Murphy had seen at the Playboy mansion. With her continuous struggles, it appeared at times, that she had on a green-and-yellow cotton belt wrapped around her waist and nothing more. People walking by were gawking and to Murphy's displeasure he was forced to call for a wagon to transport her safely and discretely. Waiting for the wagon, he continually adjusted her clothing, attempting to cover her as well as the situation would allow.

The wagon took the young lady to a nearby hospital where Murphy conferred with the doctor. He explained the situation and was informed that the doctor would move her to a room and have her psychologically evaluated. This would take a few minutes and he requested that Murphy watch her in a small conference type room until he was ready for her. She and Murphy were left alone in room and after she had calmed down he removed the cuffs from his beautiful attacker. Murphy explained that she was not under arrest, but that she would have to see a doctor before she left the hospital. This bothered her and she asked if there was any other way to settle their little problem. Standing inches from Murphy, she purred in a soft voice "I will do anything, anything you want, just let me out." Murph's only human. He couldn't take anymore temptation so he left the room explaining that he would be right outside the door and that she would have to see the doctor before she could leave. Murphy stood in the hall for a few minutes; he knew he couldn't return to that room by himself. For god's sake, Murphy was single and twenty-five years old. Anyway, after a long few minutes, the doctor returned and they both entered the conference room together to see an open window with drapes flowing in the wind. Murphy's tantalizing young woman was nowhere in sight. Murph stood there halfway between upset and relief.

She was not a prisoner, so there was no complaint. She was now an absent patient and Murph was out of there. Thirty-five years later, he remembers that day like yesterday. And he smiles.

HELIUM TANKS

In July 1993, Murphy's sergeant assigned him to patrol Lawrence Avenue between Pulaski and Kedzie to thwart gang activity in response to a recent shooting of a local businessman. After numerous uneventful trips, Murphy spotted heavy smoke in the near distance. Speeding to the scene, he arrived at a burning three flat on the corner. Shouting "Emergency" into his mike, he was immediately given the radio priority. Requesting additional police personnel, along with the fire department, Murphy began instructing the dispatcher that the first police units on the scene block off all vehicular traffic on Monticello and following units block off the alleys West and South of the building. Murphy pulled his own squad off the street and onto the lawn across from the apartment building so as not to block the incoming fire trucks. The air was blackened with rancid smoke pouring from windows, and it was obvious that this was more than the usual residential fire. Realizing the building was still occupied, Murphy ran up two flights of stairs before being met by a grandmother and two small children. Assisting them to safety, he returned after being informed that an elderly woman who lived on the top floor was not accounted for. Back into the stairwell that was now dark with smoke. He was using the walls for guidance as he quickly worked his way to the top floor where to his astonishment he found two five-foot-long tanks of helium on the landing. Understanding the potential danger of the tanks, Murphy lugged the first one down the stairs and as gently as possible dragged it across the street to safety. By then, the first fire truck had arrived on the scene. The front door flew open and Murphy was quickly briefing the fire lieutenant as the hoses were pulled and the water was charged. Eerily, the doorbell continued to buzz suggesting the old woman on the top floor was trapped. Armed with a one-and-a-half-inch hose, up the stairs they went. The fire lieutenant dragged the hose up the three flights of stairs spraying the stairwell as Murphy pulled and tugged the remaining hose behind him. As they approached the apartment where the front door had been, flames were shooting all around them lapping at the lieutenant's boots. The doorway was on fire and the inside hall was glowing with flames on both sides. Murphy shouted that he heard the crackling of the ceiling beams coming down and it was at this time the lieutenant ordered him out of the building. Before Murphy retreated, he witnessed this heroic fireman take the hose, curl it up, and throw it through the burning opening where the door once was. He then moved back into the hall way and got a running start. He dove through the burning doorway and did a barrel roll into the apartment while simultaneously grabbing the hose and soaking the walls. Murphy made his way down the stairs and onto the street attempting the catch his breath. Between sputtering and coughing, he informed the second truck on the scene that the lieutenant was on the third floor and needed assistance. Just then the second tank blew up and all eyes were focused at the front door. Moments later the lieutenant was sprinting down the stairs to safety. The fire became too intense and had to be fought from the outside. As more fire equipment arrived, the fire was eventually put out. Murphy found himself sharing a fire ambulance with the lieutenant while he took oxygen and Murphy had a small gash on his hand cared for. The man with the blacked face explained that he had to search for the old lady. Once that was accomplished he beat feet and got the hell out of there as he heard the roof giving way. As luck would have it, the occupant of the third floor was not at home when the children on the second floor accidently started the fire with matches. The buzzing noise emanating from the door bell was explained as melted wires causing a short. The fire destroyed the apartment complex, but with no fatalities. Heck of a day for the CPD and the CFD.

Part Two

THE SERGEANT

SOMETIMES YOU EAT THE BEAR, SOMETIMES THE BEAR EATS YOU

Sergeant Murphy's presence was requested in the district. A rookie police officer made an arrest of a young man for possessing a bag of marijuana. After transporting the arrestee into the district, he handcuffed him to the ring in the interrogation room of the old 17th District station.

It is customary to empty the arrestee's pockets and place the contents on the table. This way the officer could guard anything of value, as he uses the table to complete his paperwork. Believing the arrestee was secure, the officer walked to the front desk to retrieve an arrest form. Gone less than a minute, he returned in time to observe the arrestee chewing like crazy. He had taken the baggy of dope off the table and was in the process of devouring it like a rabbit eating a piece of lettuce.

After realizing his evidence was gone, the officer called Sergeant Murphy for advice. After Murph stopped laughing, he explained to the apprentice officer; "Sometimes you eat the bear, sometimes the bear eats you." Instructing him to accept this as a teaching moment, Murphy schooled him about handling items of evidentiary value. As for the arrestee, in order to avoid hospitals and stomach pumps, Murph suggested the officer release him and drive him to the nearest pizzeria or convenient store.

ARRESTING THE STUDENT BURGLAR

Working in tandem with a team of officers from a local high school, Sergeant Murphy gained information about a burglary and confirmed that the offender was a student. Further investigation revealed this student committed numerous burglaries and stored the proceeds in his school locker. After being alerted to his presence in school one day, Murphy arrived with a couple of street officers with the intentions of arresting the student. They were met at the school's entrance by the officers assigned to the school and after speaking to the attendance staff, the group headed toward the room the student burglar was in. The dean of discipline stopped them in the hall and questioned their presence in his school. Murphy explained that they were going to make an arrest of a student for a string of burglaries. The dean informed Murphy that no student would be arrested without his consent and if Murphy wanted to affect this arrest, he would have to wait until school was officially over and arrest him off school property. Murphy explained that he didn't seek his advice, nor did he need his permission to arrest a felon on school property. The dean was adamant that the police were not going to be allowed to arrest this student during class time. Standing nose to nose, Murphy explained in no uncertain terms that if he did not stand aside he would be arrested and charged with interfering with a lawful arrest. Murphy further stated he would personally handcuff him and drag him out the front doors to his squad car during class break for all the students to see. The dean stood aside and officers located themselves at the front and rear doors to the classroom. All officers simultaneously entered and handcuffed the student without issues. Murphy apologized to the teacher for the inconvenience and minutes later they were transporting their burglar into the 17th District for processing.

SUPER BURGLAR

As a sergeant assigned to the usually quiet 16th District, Murphy was working on a case of a super burglar. There were between twenty and twenty-two garages being burglarized at about 4:00 am, every third or fourth night. It appeared that the thief was knowledgeable about police schedules. He burglarized a complete city block of garages early in the morning when he knew patrol officers would be taking lunch or just relaxing after a long night shift. After taking a few days off, he would strike again, committing approximately twenty garage burglaries within less than an hour's time and then disappear. He rarely struck in the same immediate neighborhood and never showed any pattern of movement: a very professional and confusing modus operandi.

The only common denominators were garages, the early mornings, and similar items stolen. The district commander was taking a beating from the area deputy and the superintendent. All high ranking supervisors live and die on crime statistics and this was making their boss look pretty bad.

Driving separately, officers Ruby and Freddy were roaming the alleys on a cold December morning. Citizens can't comprehend what it is for officers to work full speed through the night for five or six hours until the district calms down, then slow to a snail's pace and roam the alleys without lights at three miles per hour. Viewing every garage service door and investigating every gate that is accidently left open takes its toll as officers are always on high alert. Officers have to treat each and every open gate as a bona fide incident until proven otherwise. Besides being physically tiring, the emotional stress is tremendous. This process went on every night for weeks.

At five o'clock one snowy morning, a call came in about a suspicious person in a backyard. The caller gave no further details. Officers Freddy and Ruby responded immediately. Being nearby, Murphy also responded to the call. Communicating with each other via the radio, the officers converged on the location from various directions. Officer Freddy arrived first. He approached one lit up garage and he heard a noise that sounded like a metal bar striking the concrete a couple of garages away. Murphy was seconds away when a vehicle without lights, turned out of the same alley and began slowly driving west down the street Murph was advancing on. Immediately, he activated the blue lights and pulled over a middle-aged black man. As Murphy approached the vehicle with gun in hand, the driver shouted at him that he was stopping him because he is black. Murphy responded, "I'm stopping you because you're a fucking burglar." Murphy shouted on the radio and Officers Freddy and Ruby arrived on the scene. After being removed from his vehicle, the suspicious person was handcuffed after he failed to produce a driver's license. After searching their new found friend, they recovered a cell phone that he had no explanation for, nor could he explain how it got into his pocket. They had captured their super burglar.

With a light snow covering, the alley presented a trail of unusual but similar footprints from the overhead garage doors to service doors, then back to the next garage and so on. The burglar was slick enough to enter the alley just one time at the end of the block and go to the side garage doors, then use the backyards to go from garage to garage, avoiding the alley's overhead lights. He made entry on the side door by kicking it open or prying it open with the crowbar that he initially dropped when he heard officer Freddy approach earlier. After making entry he would quickly take the stolen items and stack them in a pile on the garage apron. He then would return to the backyard and the process would start over again, garage to garage. The super burglar would repeat those steps until both sides of the entire alley were completed. With his bounty stacked and ready, he would drive his vehicle down the alley and toss his loot into the trunk. This drive would probably take a few minutes. The officers stopped him before he started loading his vehicle. The cell phone they recovered was identified as taken from a car parked inside the last garage he was spotted in. This was the evidence they needed to prove he was in at least one garage.

Murphy took the offender's gym shoes off and compared the abnormal imprint of the heel to the footprints in the newly fallen snow, they matched perfectly. The heel of his shoe had a half-moon gouge in it, probably caused from a cut from a sharp piece of glass. Murphy requested on the radio that no police officers walk down the alley as it was now a crime scene. Two evidence technicians were requested because of the amount of photography needed. As the ETs arrived on scene, Murph presented the offender's shoes and the unusual imprint in the right heel. The ET's each took one side of the alley and photographed the path taken by the burglar. Photos of the footprints left on kicked in doors were also taken, along with numerous photos of stolen property stacked neatly awaiting pickup outside each garage.

By now the sun was up and the news media was on the scene. The district commander was notified at home and gladly came into the station early. They had just caught the most wanted person in the district. The detectives were getting nowhere with the arrestee who had recently been released from Pontiac State Penitentiary after serving numerous years for burglary. There were twenty-two garages burglarized in the single alley but the state's attorney's office would only approve charges on one case of burglary. Murphy quickly notified the district commander of the hesitation on the state's attorney's part. This is when the DC hit the ceiling. He got on the phone with the state's attorney's supervisor and after some yelling and pleading; charges of six burglaries were approved. The number six was an arbitrary figure. The officers worked through the day and into the evening. They had removed from the streets of the 16th District a person responsible for more than one hundred and twenty burglaries. He was eventually found guilty and returned to his cell in Pontiac. Freddy, Ruby and Murphy were honored with being named officers of the month.

Now for the silliest thing that broke the case wide open. On the second to the last garage that he entered, the owner happened to be standing in her kitchen getting a drink of water at that early hour. A noise startled her and she observed a suspicious person outside her window. She flipped the switch and turned on the light over the garage service door while the burglar was prying it open. He apparently thought the light was on a motion detector, ignored it and continued breaking into the garage while the owner was talking to the 911 dispatcher. Moments later Murph and the crew arrived on the scene and introduced themselves to the super burglar.

GUN BUYBACK PROGRAM

The city had a unique approach in its war on guns. With donated gift cards from local merchants, the police department set up gun turn-in locations dispersed throughout the city. Many of these areas were chosen because they were the most affected by gun related violence. Murphy was a sergeant in charge of six sets of officers who were scattered across Chicago's west side, in churches and schools. Their mission was to sit in the building and accept any style of gun in return for a $50 gift card from a local merchant, no questions asked. This non-confrontational approach was to gain the trust of the people and to take the most weapons of the street as possible.

Murphy was on his second cup of coffee when he pulled up to a squad car with two officers sitting in the church parking lot. He asked why they were not in the church collecting guns. Their response startled him. The reverend from the church would not allow them to enter his church. The reverend did not like, or trust Chicago police officers. Murphy had the officers sit in the church parking lot and make the best of a poor situation. As you can see, not all battles are with the street criminals.

WHAT GOES AROUND, COMES AROUND

Sergeant Murphy returned to work after two days off, to find that their desk sergeant was injured while working the street. He sustained a serious laceration to the forehead when struck in the head with an airborne bottle. A Polish Independence Day celebration turned nasty. A drunken reveler threw a beer bottle that skipped off the top of a squad car and struck him perfectly in the forehead, opening a cut that needed immediate medical attention. The sergeant was driven to the local hospital. With a dirty rag taken from the squad car's trunk, still covering his bleeding wound, the sergeant waited thirty minutes for medical care. Receiving none, the officers removed him from the waiting area, and took him to a hospital in Park Ridge. He was immediately seen by a triage nurse, and within minutes he was being treated by a doctor. This is how an injured police officer is supposed to be treated. This was no accident, this man was injured protecting the citizens of Chicago and should be afforded the care commensurate with that unselfish duty.

Now for the rest of the story: When a person is inebriated to the point of not being able to care for themselves, by law they are to be given medical treatment. The following night while holding roll-call, Murphy ordered that all inebriated persons found on the street be taken to the hospital for medical attention. This included the normal group of street people that haven't seen a shower in weeks, that pissed their pants, and crapped themselves regularly. This order was repeated for the next couple of nights.

When an inebriant is transported to a hospital, the hospital personnel have a legal obligation to care for that person, including cleaning them up, feeding them, and of course any medical care required. As you can guess this treatment was the subject of a few discussions between Murphy and the head nurse over the next few nights.

Nobody leaves an injured police officer sitting in his own blood.

HOME INVASION

In 2004, Murphy was a field sergeant in the 17th District. A call of a suspicious person was broadcast. Officers Pat and Maureen, the district's burglary team responded using a covert vehicle. Murph was nearby and took the job in. Pat and Maureen arrived as Murphy was exiting his squad car. Pat and he, without a word being said, went opposite ways around the house as Maureen headed toward the front door. They met in the rear of the large house near a small broken window that appeared too small to enter. Their attention was drawn back to Maureen alerting the dispatcher that the front door was ajar. Pat and Murphy made their way back to the front door where Maureen was waiting. With guns drawn, they entered and began a systematic search of the seemingly vacant home. A single bedroom caught their attention because of muffled noises emanating from it. The officers took up positions on either side of the door and pushed it open with their foot to find the moaning emanating from under a bedspread. Throwing back the bedspread, they found to their amazement, an older Asian woman gagged and hog tied. Freeing her, Maureen used her calming influence to extract enough information to reveal a home invasion had taken place and she was the lone occupant. More information was gathered from the 911 call and Murphy went across the street to interview the original caller. After realizing the caller was an off-duty Chicago police officer, Murphy believed their luck was changing. Initially, he understood this incident was a home invasion perpetrated by an Asian gang and that this house was chosen very carefully and not at random. But, during Murphy's conversation with the young man, the Asian officer explained to him that he did not wish to be involved and that he would no longer speak to the police. Astounded, Murphy took a couple of deep breaths and as calmly as possible, with the veins in his neck bulging, explained to this young man that it was his duty as a police officer to assist in this ongoing investigation. And that if he failed to do so, Murphy would obtain an official complaint against him and would not stop until he got him fired.

This apparently resuscitated some of his police training and he supplied Murphy with the descriptions of the vehicle, license plates, and detailed descriptions of the suspicious persons. Officers Jim and Rich responded to the scene and relayed the newly obtained information over the various police radio zones to bordering districts.

As in all respectable police work there is good fortune, or luck as some would say. On this day, there was an attentive police officer working a bordering district monitoring his radio. He jotted down the descriptions and license plate number. A short time later he spotted the wanted vehicle at a motel on Lincoln Avenue. The officers on the scene responded and after interviewing the manager, they found to their amazement the offenders had rented two motel rooms days earlier. Having a sufficient amount of police officers on scene, officers knocked on the door and to their astonishment were met by a young Asian. As the door opened, two other Asian men fitting the description were observed sitting on the bed dividing a large amount of cash and miscellaneous jewelry. All three suspects were placed into custody and the second room was searched with more evidence being secured. An evidence technician was called and finger prints and photos were taken as well as a collection of other incriminating evidence including passports, maps, and the victim's personal schedules.

Detective Ron, an experienced and an acknowledged expert, arrived and directed the investigation from there. Over the next week, Ron worked tirelessly and put together an airtight case. The three men would be called in front of a Grand Jury, indicted and charged with home invasion, burglary, armed robbery, kidnaping, unlawful restraint, and aggravated battery to a senior citizen. The mastermind fled to California and the proper paperwork was filed to extradite him if and when he was ever located.

The investigation revealed that the male Asian from California obtained information about a thriving business in Chicago where the owner took home the proceeds because he did not trust the banks. He put together a crew and made arrangements to fly to Chicago separately and meet in a motel. Using a rented car, they invaded the owner's northwest side home looking for a reported ten thousand dollars. After repeated threats to the old woman, they were brought to a small desk in the basement. In a bottom drawer was the much sought after treasure. The home invaders also took valuable jewelry pieces as they ransacked the bedrooms. All three home invaders eventually fled through the front door to the waiting get-a-way car. Unknown to all the perpetrators, the driver remained parked in plain view of the off- duty police officer. This indeed was the lucky piece of the puzzle. The three suspects in custody pled guilty and were sentenced to long periods of imprisonment. The fourth has not faced justice as of this writing.

EASY PINCH

As Murphy has repeatedly stated, most criminals are not Einsteins. He responded to a call of "Information for the Police" at a local high school. It seemed that a student had been driving a stolen car to school for the last two weeks. Murphy asked him about it and he replied he didn't like taking the bus all the way from the south side to the north side school. It took too long and was uncomfortable. The hot car was owned by a teacher and was originally stolen from the teacher's parking lot located on the other side of the building. Jr Einstein was placed under arrest for possession of a stolen auto and transported into the district for processing.

DOCTOR DOESN'T ALWAYS KNOW BEST

After chasing and fighting with their drugged up offender, Murph and several officers finally got him handcuffed. It took six police officers to control this one person who was on PCP, an animal tranquilizer, which gives a person the sense of superhuman strength. Pain is no longer felt. Without the ability to feel pain your body does not know it's being injured, therefore there is no reason to stop doing whatever is causing the injury. This is why it took six police officers to control one person. He was now handcuffed and taken to the closest hospital for a couple of sutures for his forehead.

Now laying face up on a hospital gurney, Murph had officers standing on either side of the arrestee, holding a towel over his mouth preventing him from spitting on the officers. The experienced nurses know full well why he took this precaution. The inexperienced female doctor strolled in the room, and immediately ordered the towel removed. Murphy explained to her the reasons for the towel and she educated Murphy, "Sergeant, this is my hospital and I am in charge here." The towel was removed and as she leaned over to inspect his wound, he promptly jerked forward and with jaws clamping down, missed taking her nose off by a few inches. The towel was replaced, albeit this time by hospital personnel.

PCP AGAIN

Another individual on PCP was taken to the same hospital for treatment when the head nurse ordered the handcuffs taken off. Murphy explained the circumstances of why this person has been brought there. She made it abundantly clear that she was in charge and that the cuffs had to be removed. Seeing that this patient was not under arrest, they had no legal obligation to keep him restrained. Murphy did explain to the nurse that she should bring in her hospital security and they should be prepared to restrain him immediately.

Sergeant Murphy ordered his men, "When the cuffs are removed, I want all police personal to clear the room immediately regardless of what takes place. The hospital security is now in control of this situation." The instant the cuffs were removed, he was like a rodeo steer; the patient bucked up and down attempting to flee. The security was on him momentarily and the handoff worked well. The nurse stood by and observed. Afterward she apologized for doubting Murphy's initial judgement. All good people learn from their mistakes. Luckily, this time nobody was injured.

HELL OF A NERVE

While driving east on Irving Park at Narragansett during rush hour, Murphy spotted a cab coming westbound on the wrong side of the street. The cabbie started about a city block down and was passing about forty cars sitting in traffic waiting for the light to change. Murph flipped on the blue Mars lights and met him head on. Stopping down the block, Murphy exited his squad car and the cabbie quickly explained that he was going to enter the turning lane. Murphy corrected him loud enough so that the other drivers could hear him. He had to sit in traffic like the other rush hour drivers. As he argued his case Murphy expressed his displeasure with his maneuver. With a couple of dozen of law-abiding citizens observing, Murphy offered him the option of receiving a traffic citation, or, backing up and getting back into the proper traffic lane. With Murph's blue lights slowing traffic, the cab driver backed up a city block and eventually relocated to the end of the line. To a roaring applause and the cat calls to accompany it, Murphy happily waved to his new admirers and drove off into the sunset.

FIREMEN TO THE RESCUE

A simple traffic accident was broadcast over the radio soon followed by a frantic voice, shouting, "10-1, 10-1!" Blood pressure rises, the heart starts to race, and the hair on the back of your neck stands up. The siren started to wail and the flashing lights bounded off of the cars and buildings as sergeant Murphy raced towards the officer needing assistance. Screeching to a halt, he bailed out of the squad car to see another sergeant aiming his .9 millimeter pistol at a spaced out druggy that was slashing at the sergeant with a knife and thrusting at him with a hypodermic needle.

The crazed look on his face told the story. This guy, for whatever reason, was completely out of touch with reality. As more squad cars slid to a stop, the demented offender quickly retreated into a small vehicle that was lodged against a tree, the apparent accident. Once back inside the vehicle and no longer an immediate threat, training took over: Murphy began to direct the action. All officers who immediately surrounded the vehicle and by this time were pointing their weapons at the offender and at each other simultaneously were directed to holster their weapons. One officer was stationed on each side of the vehicle with weapons at the ready. The area was secured, a perimeter was set, traffic re-routed, and the responding fire trucks and ambulance were stationed off to the side in case a police officer got injured.

After taking a couple of deep breaths, a plan was formulated. Murphy attempted to speak to the crazed occupant but was met with him attempting to stab Murphy with the needle and slash him with the knife. Murph took out his pepper spray and soaked the lone occupant; it didn't even slow him down. Murphy emptied a lieutenant's pepper spray into the vehicle, again, didn't faze him. Officers eventually emptied nine canisters of pepper spray in this tiny two-door vehicle without any reaction from this deranged lunatic. Pepper spray doesn't work well on druggies.

They went to plan B. An officer stationed at either side of the vehicle would lure the offender to his side of the vehicle and when he reached out to stab the officer, Murphy would strike him with his night stick to disarm him or worst case scenario, disable his arm. They repeatedly went from one side to the other of the vehicle trying to incapacitate him, while attempting to eliminate the threat without using deadly force. After repeatedly striking this guy without even slowing him down, the plan was again revised.

With the permission of the field lieutenant, Murphy spoke to the firemen that originally responded to the accident call. After a few seconds to mull over the request they cheerfully dragged out their one-and-a-half-inch hose and started up the pump. At a prearranged signal, an officer ripped open the door on the far side of the vehicle. As the crazed man slid across the narrow car seat, attempting to stab the officer, Murphy flung open the door on the street side. The firemen stepped in, opened the nozzle and hit this guy with a stream of water. One hundred pounds of pressure lifted him off the seat of the car and propelled him through the air. Out of the vehicle this drugged-up superman flew. He never even touched the sidewalk. He sailed over the manicured hedge and bounced off the brick wall of the factory. Within seconds the attacker was placed in handcuffs and wondering aloud what the hell just happened.

A later investigation of this incident revealed that the driver had just purchased a speedball which is cocaine mixed with heroin. He shot up in the car which explained the hypodermic needle, then drove east just two blocks before running his Saturn up a tree on the city parkway. A Good Samaritan called the police to report the accident and initiated one of the more interesting incidents Murphy's ever been involved in.

GREAT TEAM WORK

The tactical office had received a tip from an informant that an extremely dangerous person wanted by the police would be at a pawn shop on Belmont Avenue. The intelligence gathered on this violent felon stated that he was heavily armed and would shoot it out with the police when stopped. Quickly gathering officers in civilian dress, they setup around the pawn shop. Murphy had five marked squads in alleys and nearby parking lots prepared to block all traffic on Belmont if necessary. He had pairs of undercover officers in the stores adjacent to the pawn shop. Murph was sitting across the street in a parking lot with another sergeant using binoculars to observe the front door. One of the officers spotted the offender parking his vehicle. They wanted to do the takedown but there was too much pedestrian traffic so they allowed him to continue into the pawn shop. Murphy requested that the dispatcher give them the "air" and keep all other officers off the radio. He announced to all the officers on the detail to be on their toes. After a few minutes, the felon completed his business and emerged. As he stepped onto the sidewalk, the sergeant and Murphy shouted on their respective radios to take him down. Within seconds, the streets were blocked. His attention was focused on the officers running toward him from across the street. This allowed officers from the adjoining storefronts to bum rush him and take him to the ground with him never being able to draw the .357 magnum from his waistband. Great takedown! No officers injured, one very bad guy in handcuffs, and within a few minutes the area was returned to normal. It's an unbelievable feeling when a plan of that magnitude comes to fruition. But, it pays off to work with some of Chicago's finest police officers.

A BIG MOUTH LANDS IN JAIL FOR 2 YEARS

Working a warm afternoon in the 17th, a call went out of, "Shots fired." About half of the district responded. The house in question was surrounded and Murphy entered the alley to poke around. A dog walker approached and told him about the occupants of the house firing a shotgun out the rear door. The sergeant quietly advanced behind the garage and near the rear door. He located about twenty spent shell casings on the ground and radioed this information to the units in the front of the house. Murph peeked into the rear window of the house and observed men and women in the kitchen drinking and laughing. He assigned a team of officers to attempt to gain entry through the front door while he attempted to enter the rear. Murphy knocked loudly and announced his presence while other officers observed the individuals from a side window. With officers covering him, he requested that the person on the other side of the door allow them entry. The response was, "Go fuck yourself jaggoff." After exchanging banter with the genius behind the locked door, Murphy received the information he was waiting for; the officers in the front had made entry. Keeping dimwit yelling profanities at him, the rear door eventually opened and police now outnumber the subjects inside the house. Murphy's attention was instantly focused on the conversationalist at the rear door. Murphy ordered him handcuffed. He explained that he is going to jail and Murph will think of a charge later.

Everybody was separated and searched. Murphy announced to the group that the police were aware of the shooting and that it was easier for one person to admit being the shooter and get arrested, rather than for all of the occupants to get arrested. One young man stood up and accepted responsibility. He then he took us to where he hid the shotgun under the mattress in a bedroom. He was charged accordingly and the shotgun was confiscated and inventoried. All the others were asked to leave quietly. That left Murphy's potty-mouthed friend from the back door. Ironically, as an officer was escorting him out, a cursory search of his jacket revealed four M100 fire crackers, also known as quarter sticks of dynamite in his pockets. They now had a charge to place on him.

Explosives are dangerous, so Murphy requested the Bomb and Arson Unit to come out to the scene and recover the explosive devices. A sergeant from B & A arrived on scene and Murphy requested a private chat with him. Murph apologized for wasting his time with such trivial nonsense, but he explained the conversation he had with the arrestee, who happened to be on parole for armed robbery. As part of his follow up investigation, the B & A sergeant had to interview the arrestee. After a few minutes of being called every derogatory name in the book, the sergeant surprisingly announced that he would charge the bad boy with possession of explosives by a felon, thus violating his parole. This meant their foul-mouthed friend was on the way back to the penitentiary to finish the remaining two years of his original robbery sentence.

THE BIG RAILROAD CAPER

Midnight shifts can be very boring. Generally, after the bars close the streets fold up for a couple of hours before the morning rush. About 4:30 am, on a Wednesday morning, Murphy pulled into the city's facility to gas the squad car up. The ensuing incident could have been on America's Funniest Home Videos. After gassing up, Murphy pulled his squad out of the exit gate. About fifty feet down the street, with his headlights illuminating them, were two middle-aged men, drunk as all hell. They were "tunnel vision" focused on pulling thick copper wire down from huge rolls lying alongside a railroad building. This building happened to be located twenty feet above them along the train tracks. Murph radioed for backup and sat there observing their dedication and endurance before they realized that the light that was assisting them was not coming from the moon. They spotted Murphy and the blue-and-white squad car. With comic book bulging eyes, they initiated their getaway. Murph quickly pulled the squad car within inches of the thieves. Jumping out with weapon in hand, he ordered both subjects to lie down on the asphalt. One of them immediately complied and stretched out on the street like a starfish out of water. The other decided to make a run for it to his waiting pickup truck. With the gun in hand, pointing back and forth, Murphy was shouting orders to his already surrendered thief, while standing just out of arm's reach of the other. The accomplice was now seated in the getaway vehicle attempting to start it. The truck battery pushed the starter slowly, cranking up, faster and faster with a grinding noise. Murphy shouted at the driver to surrender while still covering the prone accomplice. He defiantly stared back at Murph with those buggy eyes and continued cranking and cussing his old truck. This verbal battle went back and forth for about thirty grueling seconds. Murphy covered the prone felon but just couldn't reach the fleeing cartoon character. The old pickup coughed, sputtered, and finally came to life. Off he escaped onto Cicero Avenue just as Murphy's first backup unit arrived. Murphy motioned toward Cicero and barked over the radio a description of the wanted vehicle. Within seconds officers Danny and Stan were pursuing the copper thief south on Cicero and eventually on to the Kennedy Expressway. After a couple of short miles and a few off the expressway and back on the expressway maneuvers, his tired old vehicle decided to call it a night and came to a halt. The occupant was handcuffed and eventually reunited with his fellow thief.

With the copper thieves in custody, all involved drove into the district for a night of paperwork and laughs. With a little less to drink and a better getaway car, the thieves of the night may have pulled this copper caper off.

MEETING LOUIE

Returning to the 17th District after being absent a few years, Murphy was driving down Irving Park near Central Avenue. He looked to his right and observed a man sitting in a recliner, fully extended, in the middle of the empty parking lot, sipping on a cold beer. Murphy pulled a U-turn and drove into the parking lot. As Murph pulled alongside Louie, he was met with, "Get the fuck out of my front room." Startled, Murphy backed his squad car up and got out and reintroduced himself to Louie. Murphy explained to him that he should not yell at the police and to validate the point, Murph took the remaining four cans of beer placed them in a straight line in front of the squad car's tire. Murphy returned to car and proceeded to run them over, watching Louie's reaction as they burst. Beer and foam sprayed in all directions. Louie's expression was equal to that of a mother deer watching a wolf tear the life out of her newborn faun. Murphy explained to Louie that with a little mutual respect, they could both exist on the same streets. After that one disagreement, Louie and Murphy went on to have a symbiotic relationship. Although Louie would never become a snitch, a casual conversation with him provided you with the pulse of the neighborhood. On occasion, Murph would throw him a bone, like lunch or beer money. This was why Murphy was probably the only police officer in the district who never had to fight with Louie.

PLEASE LET IT BE A DOLL

It was seven thirty on a quiet morning. While on the way to get his morning coffee, Murphy was interrupted by the crackle of the radio. The dispatcher rarely assigned a supervisor a job this early in the shift unless it was very serious. A man walking his dog observed a small body between two apartment buildings that he described as either a doll or an infant laying on the sidewalk. Fire department was on the way. Murphy had a gut feeling this wasn't going to be good.

Being just a few blocks away Murph arrived in time to observe a fireman draping a sheet over the motionless infant's body. Accessing the situation, Murphy immediately requested that the sheet be removed and explained that the sheet could cross-contaminate the evidence of and on the tiny body. The firemen affixed the sheet along the adjoining fence to block the curious from viewing the lifeless infant.   Murphy began making notifications; the 911 dispatcher was notified that they had a body of an infant child that appeared to have just been born with the umbilical cord still attached. The watch commander was apprised and district commander soon followed. Murphy requested additional cars and detectives were notified and on their way. The district commander instantly inquired about any additional resources needed. Murphy's list was long but immediately granted. As more personnel arrived, officers surrounded the building setting up an inner and outer perimeter and with additional arrivals they cordoned off the street. Tactical teams were dispatched and directed to conduct a canvass (house to house interviews) on the block to determine if neighbors could identify any fellow neighbor who was pregnant. Additional tactical officers were sent to nearby hospitals to inquire if anybody had sought medical assistance related to childbirth. After receiving a suggestion from officer Ron, another officer was sent into the station to begin calling outlying hospitals with the same inquiry.

Murphy

In such a shocking incident like that, time disappears, situational and tactical decisions are made on the fly. There is no script to follow. And as in most horrible situations, it's hurry up and wait.

News media were arriving and becoming a nuisance as usual. Officers were sent to corral them. Murphy decided the corner two hundred feet down from the crime scene to be the logical place to keep them from obtaining any close-up pictures of the infant victim. After speaking with the on scene paramedics, it was determined that the infant, still attached to the umbilical cord, had been stabbed approximately five times in the chest. A little boy, his body was then thrown from a window above and ricocheted off the same fence that now held his privacy curtain.

Officers stationed in the rear of the apartment complex requested Murphy's presence behind the building, near the garbage dumpster. Bloody towels and what appeared to be a human placenta was found in one dumpster, which now was guarded by the inquisitive but alert officer. Additional officers were assigned to the alley as the news media now circled like vultures and attempted to video and picture the gruesome crime scene. After securing the newly found evidence and strengthening the perimeter, Murphy was given notice that sergeant Hal and his team had located the mother at a local hospital and that they were monitoring her. An arrest at this time would not be prudent seeing that the offender was a registered patient being treated in a medical facility. The sergeant and his officers maintained a presence and took the proper steps to ensure her privacy, while preventing her from escaping. This was very good news. They could now cancel the canvass that officers had been carrying out that was so vital but so draining on resources.

Murphy's watch commander, along with the district commander, requested his presence in front of the encircled building and the watch commander handed Murphy a small torn piece of paper with an address on it. She smugly explained that the mother/offender could be found there. Murphy took the torn sheet and read the address aloud, while turning to gaze upon the address affixed to the building that they were standing in front of; the same building that they had an airtight perimeter around. Murphy looked at the watch commander and crumbled up the piece of information and tossed it to the ground. Again the district commander inquired if Murphy needed any other personnel. He thanked him for his diligence and watched with anticipation as the detectives arrived on the scene.

Murph quickly briefed the detectives and explained; the building was locked down while they waited for their arrival. They had set up a perimeter and it was still intact as they arrived, and the probable offender was at the local hospital being closely monitored. They finally made entry into the three flat. They were aware that the third floor would be the likely level from which the infant was discarded. Within seconds of knocking, the door squeaked open. A middle-aged man sweating profusely instantly blurted out that his bathroom was bloody and the woman who stayed with him had left early that morning. Upon viewing the bathroom, they instantly recognized the scene of the fatal birth. Blood soaked towels and rags littered the floor. Bloody scissors were secreted behind the toilet and items with blood stained finger prints lined the small bathroom window.

The crime lab (major crime investigators) arrived on scene and processed the evidence for presentation in court. It was later determined that the small scissors found in the bathroom was used to cut the umbilical cord, then to stab the infant five times in the chest before the disoriented mother threw her newborn son out the third story to his imminent death.

The mother, who originated from Guatemala, was arrested and charged with murder. The infant was laid to rest in a proper Catholic funeral, with the casket and flowers being donated by a local funeral home and florist. The funeral procession was mostly composed of community members and Chicago police officers.

Every officer on the crime scene or at the funeral went home that night and hugged their children. The mother was eventually convicted of murder and sentenced to a lengthy term in the penitentiary.

UNUSUAL BURGLARY

Sergeant Murphy was new to the district and to the rank of sergeant as well. Knowing what power a sergeant of police really held was soon to be discovered.

Pulling his squad car to the rear parking lot of a bank alarm was the easiest part of the job. About five o'clock in the morning, with the moon still offering light, Murphy easily detected the ladder propped against the brick wall. Requesting additional units, Murphy didn't know if the offenders were still on the roof, in the bank, or anywhere else for that matter. Directing squad cars to the front parking lot on Foster Avenue with additional units to set the perimeter around the Harlem Ave side, the police response to the bank alarm was excellent.

Once a perimeter was set, Murphy and a few officers climbed the twenty-foot ladder to the roof. A two-by-two-foot hole was cut through it with a rope ladder swinging freely to the bank floor. A sledge hammer, torches, and various other construction tools were scattered around the roof.

Bank officers were notified and arrived on the scene almost instantaneously. The front door was opened and a squad of officers entered into the unexpected. Quickly searching every inch of the bank, the "all clear" was given.

Murphy began to collect further information from the bank manager. They viewed the hole in the false ceiling together and the bank manager revealed a startling piece of news. There were two ceilings in the building: One for the bank, but above that was a ceiling that led throughout the entire building. That building happened to be the entire shopping mall located at Foster and Harlem. To add to the excitement, there was noise emanating from various parts of the ceiling, like groaning or scraping. It was possible the offenders were trapped in the ceiling, maybe the air ducts. It gets better; Murphy soon found out that there were two separate systems of air ducks throughout the bank's ceiling. The police presence just expanded. A new perimeter was set around the entire shopping mall/building. The sun replaced the moon and people were arriving for work. Officers were stationed at various points informing employees to refrain from entering their respective stores. Back in the bank, a police officer had stripped off his leather jacket and shirt was now crawling through the ventilation system with pistol and flashlight, his partner walking below him.

No officers could be spared so man power changes from the midnight watch to the day watch were conducted in the bank parking lot. The day shift field lieutenant arrived on the scene and requested Murphy release some cars to their assigned schools crossings. Understanding the manpower drain, Murphy explained the need for the full police presence. There was a slim chance that the bank burglars were still secreted in the false ceiling or the ventilation system of the bank, and as such, possibly throughout the entire building. This likelihood was small, but would the lieutenant risk his position if a burglar fell through the bank's false ceiling onto the bank president's desk after they pulled the officers out? The lieutenant allowed Murphy the army of police required to properly complete the mission.

After a thorough search of the ceilings and both of the ventilations systems, the all clear was once again given. The perimeter detail was thanked and released. Officers protecting the roof and ladder turned control over to the waiting evidence technician and went home. The paper car completed the reports and used the bank's copy machine to supply the follow up detectives with the collected information. Sergeant Murphy returned to the district to brief the on-coming watch commander of the entire incident, including the loss from the ATM machine inside the bank that was the target of the break in.

In a situation like that, a decision has to be made on the amount of man power to use. Too much and you waste it, too little and the goal at hand may never be achieved. A sergeant has great leeway in his assessment of man power usage. Since that assignment, on various other occasions sergeant Murphy has requested the use of the helicopter, the police boat, the fire department boat, dive teams, K-9 units, the SWAT team, the SORT team, FBI, State Police, various suburban police departments, and a myriad number of city and state services. The bank burglary did not produce an arrest, but it certainly did educate Sergeant Murphy.

BROKEN HEART

One icy cold January night, Murphy's presence was requested at a domestic disturbance involving very young children. He met with the beat officers assigned to the call, and they quickly brought him up to speed about the situation. Standing in the street was an expressionless woman. On the sidewalk was a young man offering his fatherly viewpoint to any police officer who would listen. They were the parents of two very young babies and had recently separated. She went her way and he stayed in the apartment to care for the children, one being sick enough to require medication. She was staying on the west side and he was working daily and tending the children at night. She was binging on drugs and alcohols and he was reading bedtime stories while cooking and cleaning. The children were in a secure, loving environment and the mother was without transportation, medicine, or baby supplies.

The decision to be made was the most difficult police related decision Murphy would ever be faced with in thirteen years of being a sergeant of police. The mother, after a month-long absence, rode the "L" train to the north side on this bitter January night to reclaim her babies. The father supplied food, clothing, medicine, and security. The mother offered nothing but a misplaced yearning to be a parent again. As repulsed as he was, Murphy directed the officers to return the babies to the mother. In the State of Illinois, the mother has legal custody when there is no direction from a court of law. She was a hideous mother and the father was nurturing and loving, but the law is the law. The mother was not intoxicated at the moment, nor did she appear to be under the influence of narcotics. Murphy was compelled to make a decision that would haunt him for years. The father was advised to contact an attorney and initiate child custody procedures. Murphy instructed the officers to drive the mother and children to any location she wanted. On this miserable, frigid, January night, Murphy had to order two Chicago police officers, both fathers themselves, to have a caring and loving father surrender his sick children to an uncaring and seemingly unloving mother.

Fifteen years later, this decision still haunts Murphy.

A DANGEROUS WAKE

A local funeral parlor had an unusual wake one Saturday. A gang member from outside the district was shot and killed. The wake and funeral was to be held in sergeant Murphy's district for safety sake. Word on the street was there would be shooting before, during, and after the wake.

A tactical plan was put into motion using information gathered by the Chicago Police Department's Gang Intelligence Unit. A field lieutenant was placed in charged along with sergeant Murphy and sergeant Buck, a cagey and wily old veteran. Two full gang teams and an assorted number of beat cars and response cars were also allocated to this mission.

Mourners started gathering for the wake in late afternoon. A marked squad car was stationed in front of the funeral parlor and other squad cars were assigned to patrol an eight block area. Unmarked tactical units stationed down the block were busy collecting license plate numbers and running them on portable computers. They passed this collection of information to other tactical units who made car stops on selected individuals. Other marked squad cars were secreted five and six blocks away; these would become chase cars if needed.

Things were going smoothly until mourners started congregating in front of the funeral home presenting an irresistible target for rival gang members. Calls of shots fired started taking over the police radio. As things became more dangerous sergeant Buck called in reinforcements. With two squads of police officers, they shut down the wake. Buck spoke to the funeral director and declared an emergency. The mother of the deceased was notified and all mourners were escorted from the building. Officers on the outside moved the crowd and the streets were shut down to allow the gang members to evacuate the immediate area.

With peace restored the sergeants found themselves in front of the casket embracing the guest of honor. Sergeant Buck immediately began to riffle through the casket and under the body. Pulling out a deck of cards, bags of weed and bottles of various liquors; a knife and a pair of dice were also removed. No other weapons were found. The wake was declared over.

Calm once again fell over the district. All officers assigned were released and allowed to return to their respective duties. The following day had a large police presence and went well. The gang member was laid to rest with the dignity offered one in his position.

AN HONORABLE MAN

As the dispatcher was broadcasting the house fire, Murphy immediately recognized it was going to be a bad one. Drowning out the dispatcher's voice were the many fire department sirens racing in from all directions. That only meant that the house was burning like all hell. Murphy hurried with lights and sirens, and started to make his turn onto the street when he realized they had a major problem. The street was excavated the entire length of the block. It's a foot deep where the street once was; they were in the process of putting in a new sewer system. This meant the fire trucks had to park on Irving Park and struggle with rush hour traffic speeding by. Murphy observed the first truck and engine pull to a stop. Firemen bailed out of the cabs. They grabbed equipment and started to trudge down the gravel street toward the fireball looming in the middle of the block. Other trucks were arriving and pulling hose, while CFD supervisors were yelling into their fire radios, requesting more assistance. Murphy was shouting over the sounds of the fire department pumper, requesting additional officers for traffic control. Firemen getting their equipment were playing a very dangerous cat and mouse game of dodging rush hour traffic. Irving Park was now down to one impatient lane eastbound, and it was a narrow lane at that. Murphy was shouting directions over the radio ordered Irving Park Road shut down completely. It was becoming a very dangerous scene with rush hour traffic, January weather, and sunset, all coming together to form the perfect storm. And, Murphy hasn't even made it to the fire scene yet.

The whirl of the rotor blades alerted him to the fact that the news choppers were above. News trucks and cameras were popping up everywhere. The house was a fireball and the firemen are spraying the adjoining buildings. A soot covered fireman carrying a lifeless naked body emerged from the house. He found an unoccupied spot on the front sidewalk and immediately started mouth to mouth resuscitation. Arriving paramedics quickly raced to her side and administered the required medical attention, while the news media started advancing with their cameras. The elderly lady was lying on the ground while the medics attempted to revive her, ignoring the fact that she was naked. Understanding that this was someone's grandmother, Murphy pushed the camera crews back as far as he could. As the struggle between life and death played out, the news people continually inched closer. Murphy summoned Officer Scott, a retired marine sergeant. He pointed at one overly persistent photographer who insisted on videotaping this lifeless naked grandmother. He instructed Officer Scott to disrupt the man's ability to videotape the dying woman. "Aye Aye, sir," and off he went. Murphy's concentration was again directed toward the fire and supporting the fire department. Fire hoses were stretched for blocks in either direction taking on the appearance of an octopus. Pedestrian traffic was kept to a minimum but large crowds were gathering. Every time Murph was able to steal a look back at the belligerent news man, Scott was positioning and re-positioning himself in front of the man's camera lens. Scott stands six feet tall and with the police hat on, making him a very impressive and determined force to overcome.

The fire was eventually struck and the woman was transported to the nearest hospital in critical condition. She was pronounced dead at the hospital. Video footage of the fire made all the local news stations, but no video of her was seen. Officer Scott did an extraordinary job. No family should ever see their loved one dying on television, particularly under such sensitive conditions. Semper Fi, Scott.

SOME THINGS JUST WORK OUT!

Responding to a call of an auto accident on the Kennedy Expressway, Murphy arrived to find that a car had lost control and careened up the embankment through the brick wall of a storage building. The building took its toll on the old station wagon full of out-of-state vacationers. Chicago Fire Department ambulances continued to arrive until the mother and three children were provided medical assistance. The father was not injured; his youngest son had minor injuries and was scheduled to go to a local hospital. The mother and two other children were critically injured and were destined for Illinois Masonic Hospital, a very fine trauma center. All were to survive, albeit at different locations miles apart. Chicago Fire Department protocol dictates the types of medical facility injured people are taken to according to the seriousness of their injuries. As an example, it is against fire department rules to transport a patient to a trauma center if he can be treated at another facility. This rule protects the trauma centers from being overrun with lesser, non-life threatening injuries.

The dilemma: the father was without transportation and being unfamiliar with Chicago, found himself in a horrible position. Should he go to the nearby local hospital with his youngest son or to the trauma center with the more seriously injured wife and other children? Murphy assured this distraught father that they would have his automobile, full of family possessions, towed to a nearby facility that was enclosed and protected. He also would have him transported to whatever location he chose.

Murphy spoke to the CFD supervising officer on the scene and explained the dilemma the father faced. He understood and professed he could not ignore procedure and that he was forced to divide the family up among hospitals. Murphy implored him one last time if there was any way around this rule and he left Murphy standing on the embankment as he walked away. A couple of minutes later, he returned and informed Murphy that for some unknown reason the youngest child was now showing signs of head trauma and had to be directed to the same trauma hospital as the rest of the family. He took it upon himself to declare the child in need of trauma medical attention because he found an 'invisible' bump on the boy's head.

The entire family was transported by numerous Chicago Fire Department ambulances to the same hospital, followed directly by a Chicago Police Department squad car with the father. His automobile was towed to a nearby fenced in parking lot owned by some unknown Good Samaritan who protected it until the father could make plans to have it towed for repairs. The officers wrote various instructions and directions for the out-of-state visitors and Murphy made them available to the father for whatever he requested. It's a nice feeling when a plan comes together.

IMPORTANT PHONE CALL

A lieutenant, a preacher and a devoutly religious man, was holding roll call. After roll call began, the noise of a ringing cell phone rebounded off the walls. Nobody could decipher where the annoying ringing was coming from until an officer walked across the room to his backpack. Roll call stopped, everybody stared. The officer unzipped his backpack and removed the phone announcing to the lieutenant that he had to take the call. The officer left the room with the phone pushed against his ear listening intently. As the mild-mannered lieutenant resumed roll, he was once again interrupted as the officer walked back into the room. This time the officer declared to the lieutenant that he had to take the call because it might have been about "puss." The lieutenant's face turned a crimson red, the air became very heavy and you could hear a pin drop. With that said the officer bounded across the room and took up his vacated seat. Roll call was over.

A POUND OF GRASS AND THE DISTRICT COMMANDER

A sergeant's main function is to protect his men. With that said, the brakes on officer Ron's squad car were bad enough to cause concern, so he limped into the area garage. The officer, being a dependable young man, decided to use the squad car's blue lights to apprise other motorists that they should afford him the right of way, eliminating excessive breaking. This plan went awry when he collided with another vehicle at a four-way stop sign. The accident report was written and sent through to the district commander for his approval, a requirement of all accidents involving police department vehicles.

The 17th District had a "real street police officer" for district commander. After his review, he met with Murphy in the watch commander's office and directed him to proceed with disciplinary actions for the officer. Murph explained to the district commander that his function in this incident was to find a less punitive course of action and the DC agreed, allowing Murph a few days to research alternatives.

They met again in the watch commander's office. Murphy presented his oral argument that a squad car with activated lights has the right of way in any situation; therefore the officer should be free from any attached punishment. The district commander explained that the excuse of the blue lights was faulty. State law precludes this defense when the police vehicle is not in emergency operation. Murph responded that a vehicle on the right, arriving at a four-way stop, has the right of way, regardless of what type of vehicle is involved. The DC would take this new information under advisement. A few days went by and the district commander and Murphy once again met in the watch commander's office. He explained that the Illinois Traffic Laws disagreed with Murph's presumption and that he should initiate punishment. Murphy requested additional time and it was granted. Days later, he again met the district commander outside the watch commander's office and Murphy inquired if he would like a cup of coffee and a piece of birthday cake. Somebody brought in a birthday cake for a desk officer; the DC replied, "No thank you. Please initiate the punishment procedure." Murphy once again requested an extension and it was granted. Their next meeting was now into the Christmas season and Murphy heard rumors that the district commander was having out-of-town family visit him for the holidays. Murphy asked about this and the DC informed him that his relatives from down south were staying with him for a week to celebrate Christmas. Murphy suggested he supply him with a nice bottle of wine for the occasion. He declined and requested that Murphy institute disciplinary actions. A last ditch effort was required.

The following day, bright and early, Murphy met with the district commander in the usual spot, the watch commander's office. Coincidentally, tactical officers in the interrogation room were inventorying four one-pound bags of marijuana recovered during an early morning drug raid. Running out of arguments, Murphy pitched his final plea to the district commander in front of a sergeant and a new lieutenant. Murphy started with, "It was the Christmas season and we all enjoy celebrating with our family and friends." Looking directly into the district commander's eyes, Murph asked, "Would you like a pound of marijuana to celebrate with?" Without missing a beat he replied, "Murph, thirty years ago I might have, but not now thank you. Now go write up that disciplinary report." The old-time sergeant just smiled and shook his head. The new lieutenant turned bright red and Murph thought he was going to pass out. Murphy nodded and smiled to the district commander, then left the room to start his report. Thanks, Sam. You were a great boss.

GOOD OLD-FASHIONED ASS KICKING

Sergeant Murphy's watch commandeer called him into the district and asked him to oversee the station activity while he went to lunch. Rarely did he ever leave the station to eat lunch; today was the exception and what an exception it was going to be. As Murphy was standing at the desk, a beat car brought in a subject to post a simple traffic bond. He was driving without a driver's license and needed to post a bond in order to leave the station. He was overly agitated and boisterous to the point of almost getting more than he bargained for. By now, he was handcuffed to the wall in the interrogation room while the officers completed their paperwork. The arrestee was angrily shouting and screaming at the officers, so Murphy decided to intervene before this insignificant situation grew out of control.

Murphy spoke to this rather large Puerto Rican gang banger and explained the need for him to cooperate with the officers, so he could leave as quickly as possible. After appearing to calm down, he was escorted to the front desk to sign the required paperwork and he would be free to leave. After affixing his signature to the bond slip, he stood there for a few seconds gazing around. He observed the new crew coming from the roll call room and making their way to collect their radios. He caught the eye of one of the young Hispanic officers and flashed him a gang sign. With that Murphy grabbed him by the arm, another police officer grabbed his other arm and they began to escort him out the front door. He took five steps and flung his arms back, striking the other officer in the face. It was like the bell rung, the fight was on. After a few punches and jabs, they bounced off the front doors. Winding up in a pile, they started tumbling down the stairs in the vestibule of the old 17th District station. Murphy was on the bottom sliding down the stairs, while the group was riding him like a sled. One officer was punching the crap out of the offender while Murph sees Officer George reaching for his pepper spray. The word "Don't" just left Murphy's lips when they all got a splash of pepper spray. Bouncing down one stair at a time, Murph now sees Officer George's radio pop out of its holder. George drew the radio back and before Murph could say "No," he laid it across the guy's head. Murphy was still pinned under the group, the one officer is smacking the daylights out of this guy while Murphy was attempting to place handcuffs on him. Sliding all the way down the stairs, the guy was upside down now. Murphy sees a clearing and reaches for this guy's arm. He also sees George draw back his foot and, you guessed it, before he could say "No" he kicked this guy in the head. Being stunned, they now rolled him over and handcuffed him. He was carried directly to a cell. Only four officers were actually involved in the melee because of the small dimensions of the vestibule they were in. No officers were injured. They opened the doors to allow the paper spray to dissipate and Murphy headed inside to start the paper work.

Checking the clock, he decide not to notify the luncheoning watch commander because he was probably already on his way back. Instead, Murphy completed his portion of the paperwork. Just then, the lieutenant entered the building. Murphy quickly briefed him about the situation, and advised him to interview the arrestee before his eyes shut. One was already closed from the combination of pepper spray and a good thumping.

The lieutenant entered the lock up and interviewed the arrestee. Murphy waited impatiently in the watch commander's office. Not knowing what to expect, Murph was a bit nervous. The lieutenant came out from the lock up, bent over from the waist, with his hands on his hips, laughing hysterically. Murphy asked him what was so funny and he replied, "Murph, I ain't seen a beaten like that in years".

The paper work was completed and Murphy returned to the safety of the streets.

ANSWER THE PHONE

While working the street, Murphy decided to stop in the station to see what was going on. He was standing at the desk and the phone rang. Naturally he answered it. The conversation went something like this:

Murphy: "16th District, how may I help you?"

Caller: "I want to beef about one of your fuckin police men."

Murphy: "We don't make pizzas here."

Caller: "You don't understand, I want to beef about one of your fuckin police men." Murphy: "You don't understand, we don't make any pizzas here."

Caller: "Buddy, you don't understand what I'm saying; I want to complain about a police man."

Murphy: "Buddy, You don't understand what I'm saying; we don't make any fuckin pizzas here."

Click. He hung up.

JUST GIVE THEM THE BEER

Murphy was around the corner when the call came out about a woman screaming for help. Within seconds, he pulled into the alley and jumped out of the squad car. He trotted into the gangway listening intently, attempting to pick up any little sign of a woman in distress. A noise caught his attention about three flights up. As Murphy began up the stairs, he realized the noise being heard was actually a cat. He disregarded all units responding and walked back to his vehicle. Murphy spoke briefly to the tactical officers who also responded and he explained the cat crying on the porch sounded like a woman crying. All was good and he bid them a safe night. Murphy was attempting to re-enter his squad car when he realized he had locked the keys in the car and it was running. After calling the tact team on the radio, they returned and were nice enough to go into the district and retrieve the spare set of keys. They returned quickly and one officer jiggled the key out the window as she was requesting a reward of a six-pack of beer for her trials and tribulations. She kept reaching the key ring out and pulled it back as they discussed the reward. Finally, Murphy acquiesced. He said would buy them a six-pack for their troubles. She smiled and handed him the keys. Murphy immediately shouted that their six-pack would come over his dead body. Murph laughed as he lumbered back to his car. He pushed the spare key into the door lock only to have it _not_ unlock the door. Confused he looked up to see the officer offering another set of keys to him. Laughingly she explained that the keys they gave him were not the keys to his car. But if Murphy really wanted the true set of keys, the promise of the beer would have to be fulfilled. Checkmate. To this day they laugh about how Murphy got hosed in the alley.

UNJUST PUNISHMENT FOR A TRAFFIC ACCIDENT

Sergeant Murphy responded to a traffic accident involving a police car with no injuries. As Murph exited his squad car, he was approached by one of the officers from the damaged squad. He requested a private talk. Walking away from the scene of this very minor incident, Murphy asked what was so important. He responded that he was working with a recruit and that the recruit was driving. He understood the microscope that the recruits were under before they came off of probation and he requested that in the report the sergeant make him the driver. He was willing to take any blame and accompanying punishment. Technically, there was no difference of who was driving. Murphy had already determined that the police car was at fault which meant the city was liable for the minor damage on the victim's vehicle. The only unresolved issue was the punishment to be determined and to whom. The recruit technically faced discharge from the police department while the officer faced loss of a day's pay from his paycheck. Sergeant Murphy saluted the officer for having the balls to protect his partner and made him the driver.

Down the line, Murphy received direction that he was to administer punishment to this now highly appreciated officer and he wrote the paperwork without a flaw. The sergeant placed this disciplinary paperwork in the back of his locker and kept deflecting questions about it. He suggested that he had turned it in and the front office had probably lost it. Six months later, when his transfer was approved, Murph called for a meeting with the admired officer and bestowed upon him the complete file that had been "lost."

If Murphy ever accomplished anything in his career, it was helping the truly good police officers. Now, more than two of us know this story.

DIFFERENT VIEWPOINTS OF SAFETY

Driving through the 17th District one rainy evening, Murphy drove by a beat car making a traffic stop on a horde of gang bangers. He turned around and stopped to assist them. Murphy exited his squad to observe one officer searching the stopped vehicle, as the second officer stood guard over four subjects with their hands resting on the squad car. Murphy immediately sensed the potential for danger and ordered the four to kneel on the wet pavement and place their hands on the car. All complied and the sergeant felt safer. Within seconds, sergeant Howard pulled on the scene. He exited his squad car and immediately ordered the four to lay prone on the damp street and spread their arms. They again complied and everybody felt even safer.

After the traffic stop was completed and the bangers were back on their merry way, the sergeants and the officers discussed the stop. All four of them had very different perceptions of safety. Murphy agreed with Sergeant Howard, that it's your personal comfort level; you use and do whatever it takes to secure the situation. Never worrying about complaints is part of the job.

BROTHER AND SISTER UNITED

Being very short-handed, the watch commander refused to allow officer Scott to use compensatory time to visit with his sister who was in town for a few days. He had not seen his sister for many years. Being Scott's immediate supervisor and understanding that he could not disregard the standing orders of his watch commander, Murphy directed Scott to come to work at the normal time. Once at work, Murphy requested a time due slip for seven hours and sent Scott home. A brother had a long awaited reunion with his sister.

Another time due situation arose when sergeant Murphy was forced to pair a very good and hard-working police officer with a lazy ass dog. He hated to do it, but the dog-ass, who was absolutely useless, was working alone because his steady partner took the day off. The working officer stopped just short of begging for Murph to replace him, but his hands were tied, although he never stopped thinking about him. After roll call was over and the officers hit the street, Murphy called for a meeting with this particular car. He informed the officer that his seven-hour time due request was reviewed and accepted, he could leave at any time. He looked at Murph puzzled and officer dog-ass drove him back to the station and dropped him off. He thanked Murphy the following day. He never requested time due.

A CITIZEN'S GRATITUDE

Think about that brutal day. That real icy, rainy, slushy day that you wouldn't be caught dead driving in. Now add a burglary in progress to that scenario. Throw in a foot chase.

Sirens blaring and blue lights cutting through the light fog, Sergeant Murphy was responding to the burglary call. Cars were coming in from all directions and driving was extremely treacherous to say the least. The first car on the scene was now in a foot chase with a burglar.

Pushing on the gas pedal when the squad stopped sliding was the technique used. Already going too fast for conditions Murphy pushed harder. Minutes in this situation seemed like hours. The need to help this police officer diminished the anxiety in steering this three thousand pound bullet.   Eventually arriving a block down from the scene and now actively pursuing the felon, Murphy slid on the icy sidewalk. Choosing to run through the deeper snow for better traction, Murphy and the officer eventually caught their burglar. No struggle or fight was offered and the subject was handcuffed and all involved trudged back to the crime scene.

Back at the house, the rear door was kicked in and entry made. Officers on the scene had already searched and cleared the house. Proceeds were stacked up and a small amount of jewelry was recovered from the offender. Located a short distance down the alley was a stereo and television set secreted behind a garbage can. Great arrest by Chicago's finest, particularly on such a horrible and miserable day.

The neighbor had already contacted the home owner at work and she was on the way. Believing that she would be overjoyed with the police, sergeant Murphy waited anxiously.

The victim arrived and immediately informed Murphy that she didn't want to press charges. She had called a friend of hers who was a police officer and he talked her out of becoming a complainant. The court dates and the messy interviews with the states attorney, not counting the days missing work. She did not want to sign complainants. She simply wanted her things back and let the insurance pay for her broken door.

Murphy was outraged. He explained the danger the police officers put themselves and others through. He explained that it was her civic duty. He explained about the repercussions of his officers putting hands on this person. She couldn't care less. She wanted her shit back and that was it.

Instead, Murphy ordered the found stereo equipment, along with the television be taken into the district and inventoried as found property. The same went for the jewelry and change found in the burglar's pockets. It was explained to the victim that if she did not sign complaints for burglary, Murphy considered the recovered items found property and all was to be inventoried as such. If she had proof of ownership, she and her attorney could go to court and claim the found property.

The burglar was released. The victim was furious. Murphy was livid. Officers had risked their lives in an excellent police effort under some very treacherous weather conditions. So much for citizen support.

BAD CAPS MEETING

Murphy attended his very first community meeting as a sergeant in the 16ᵗʰ District. Murphy was fully prepared for the meeting because of extensive CAPS instruction in the police academy during his sergeant's training. When he walked into this meeting at Oriole Park there were about two hundred people waiting for him. Generally at a community meeting, if there are twenty people that's a lot. Two hundred people meant major issues. As Murphy introduced himself as the new CAPS Sergeant for the beat, he was met with skepticism and outright anger. Murphy didn't know the prior sergeant, but he certainly set the table for Murph, and not in a good way

It appeared there was a drug house in the district. It was sandwiched between a police lieutenant's house and an attorney's house. The good citizens allowed Murphy a few minutes to declare that he was going to take care of the situation before they jumped down his throat in unison. Murphy was informed, ever so coarsely, that they didn't believe a single word he said. The attorney called him a liar after Murphy declared the drug house would be eliminated within a week. Mr. attorney shouted that the 16ᵗʰ District police would not and could not handle this problem. Sergeant Murphy explained that he was new to the beat and the district itself, and that he would direct all his available resources to this issue until it was eliminated. Murphy's first CAPS meeting as a sergeant sucked, but he escaped with his life

Within the first twenty-four hours, Murphy composed a three-page memo to the district commander relaying the concerns of the meeting, requesting certain resources, and outlining the course of action that would be taken. The following night Murphy paid a visit to the house with a tactical team. He introduced himself to an elderly woman, who turned out to be the grandmother of the dope dealer. Murphy had a very warm and cozy conversation with her, her granddaughter and grandson. He explained that he intended to put the grandson in jail for ten years and then seize the house as a continuing house of ill repute. The granddaughter was simply advised to move.

The following night, directly out of roll call, Murphy went to the house with a wagon and three squad cars. Alongside the house was a very nice barbeque area with picnic tables, loud music, and soft lighting. They arrested everybody who was sitting around for disorderly conduct and a breach of the peace: Murphy advised them never to return. He explained that if they did return at any time, for any reason, they would again wind up in jail. The grandson was charged with possession of cocaine and underage drinking. For the following couple of nights Murph stationed a squad car to sit in front of the house and shine the squad car's spotlight into the front window. Tactical cars were used to arrest anybody who came near the house on foot or in vehicles.

Within days, the dope house closed. The grandson moved out. The granddaughter found religion, and grandma was left in peace. The dope house was eliminated within one week like promised.

The following CAPS meeting had about fifteen people, one being the attorney. At the end of this very quiet and uneventful meeting, he approached Murphy with a big smile and extended his hand saying what a fine job the police did. Murphy replied, "Go fuck yourself." He stammered, "What did you say?" Murphy again responded by saying, "Go fuck yourself." Murph refreshed the attorney's memory that he called the police officers bums and liars the first time he'd ever met him. Murphy explained that he wasn't very pleased with his attitude. Murphy said that he belittled him in front of two hundred people therefore he should apologize to him and his officers in front of two hundred people.

The following day, sergeant Murphy received a request from the district commander to have a chit-chat with him. The topic of discussion was 'did Sergeant Murphy tell the attorney to go fuck himself'? Proudly Murphy explained his conversation and readily admitted to the DC what was said. Murphy was asked to refrain from such talk and he responded that he was a proud man and also proud of his men. Murphy never received the apology, but he did get a reprimand from his boss.

MAN WITH A GUN

The local elementary school day was interrupted after a man with a gun chased another armed man through the school yard. The original call came out "Man with a gun." Murphy happened to be close by, so he took the job in. Within moments, Murph skidded to a stop just down from the location and after seeing men in the front yard with guns, he unholstered his .45 automatic. As he approached on foot taking cover behind parked cars he was ordering the guns to be dropped. The men began shouting "U.S. Marshals!" Showing identification, they were indeed United States Marshals serving an arrest warrant at that location. Once they hit the front door, an armed man fled through the rear door and down the alley. After a brief foot chase the man was captured without any shots being fired.

After the situation calmed down and everybody was determined to be safe, Murphy commenced to rip into the U.S. Marshal in charge. Raising his voice to a shout, Murphy explained how easily this mission could have gone south. With Chicago Police racing to the scene of a call of this type, any of the Marshals could have been shot or responding officers could have been injured. As Murphy was leaving the scene, still very upset, the Marshal called him over to apologize. Monitoring the radio, Murphy's watch commander contacted him on the phone. His orders were to verbally admonish the U. S. Marshal in charge. Murph explained he had already taken that liberty. All involved were very lucky that nobody was injured in that potentially very dangerous situation.

THE MISSING CELL PHONE

After brutally demanding meeting with the local Alderman and his political cronies, the district commander instructed Sergeant Murphy to furnish the beat officers with a cell phone provided by the alderman's office. Now the alderman's constituents could call the beat officers directly for issues pertaining to their neighborhood. They no longer had to go through the normal procedure of calling 911 and speak to a police dispatcher. Murphy realized that tying a beat car down to the every whim and fancy of the proverbial crazy lady in the neighborhood would completely remove those officers from any real police work. Begrudgingly, he handed the cell phone to beat Officer Curt. He instructed him, per orders from the district commander; he needed to respond to the needs of the citizens on the beat. When the tour of duty was over he was to pass the cell phone on to the next crew with the same instructions.

A week went by and Murphy followed up on the progress being made with the new procedure. The cell phone was missing. Officer Curt and his partner searched the squad car to no avail, the phone was gone. Murph submitted a short report and it was quickly forgotten.

A few days later, after a particularly warm evening, a group of officers stopped at the local watering hole for a cold beer. The subject of the cell phone came up. Officer Curt smiled and informed Murphy that immediately after receiving the cell phone the night of the meeting, he drove directly to the river and threw it in. He didn't think it was a good idea for a beat car to bypass the 911 dispatcher and be at the beckoned call of civilians, so he took it upon himself to correct the situation. Murphy smiled, bought a round of beers and congratulated him on his resourcefulness.

IT CAN HAPPEN

The paramedics were responding along with Sergeant Murphy and a paper car. On the scene, the paramedics tried franticly, but lost the battle to save the man's life. It was a heroin overdose. What made this one so very different was that the victim was in his fifties and the long time live-in boyfriend of a police officer. The home was in an upscale neighborhood, very nicely decorated and spotless. As the paramedics worked on this man's last few minutes of life; the off-duty PO made a half-hazard attempt to remove the hypodermic needle and syringe. Murphy gently reminded her that she needed to leave everything as it was. He declared the front room a crime scene and ordered a police officer to guard it. 'It' included the needle as well as the spoon used to cook the heroin, the empty baggy with heroin residue and other various paraphernalia.

The evidence technician took photos and collected the drug paraphernalia. The coroner's office requested the body and it was delivered by the wagon; then, the off-duty police officer was left to the arrangements. She was told by Murphy that no one involved would speak of that incident again. What the department didn't know wouldn't hurt them. The death of her loved one was punishment enough. Murphy suggested that if she informed his mother and siblings that he succumbed to a heart attack, no one would be the wiser. As the live-in girlfriend, she would be treated like the spouse and she would be in control of the death certificates. Murphy extended his condolences and returned to patrol.

THEY'RE CHICKENS, JUST FRIGGIN CHICKENS

Another sergeant backed Murphy up on a disturbance call at a fast food chicken restaurant. PETA, the People for Ethical Treatment of Animals, was demonstrating outside the restaurant and causing a commotion. When Murphy arrived, he informed them that they have a constitutional right to picket, as long as they abide by the laws. He informed the restaurant management about the same restrictions; they can't block traffic, pedestrian on the sidewalks or vehicular in the driveway. Picketers can't go on private property and they have to keep moving at all times. Blah, blah, blah. With that said, the sergeant and Murphy returned to their respective squad cars and left. Within minutes, they were called to return. The picketers were now blocking the driveway attempting to prevent cars from entering the restaurant parking lot. Murphy again explained the rules of picketing and they seemed receptive. Murph left. Minutes later the dispatcher sent him back to the scene. The PETA people were now pounding on the large glass windows, antagonizing the restaurant's patrons, including scaring small children. Murphy calmly called the group around him into a football type huddle and screamed, "They're chickens, just fuckin chickens!" He explained in very ordinary street language that if any police had to come back there for any reason, the paddy wagon would be backed up and everyone there would go to jail. Apparently his little speech did the trick: no more calls.

DON'T GET EVEN, GET REVENGE

Halloween is always an interesting time for a police officer. This particular night sergeant Murphy was patrolling the side streets in the 17th District. In the middle of the street, directly in front of him, was a vehicle that had been hit with a few eggs. Four teenagers were standing in front of a house that had also been egged. Murphy exited the car and requested their version of what had taken place. They explained that the people in the house had recently egged their car as they drove by and that they were now repaying the favor. This seemed fair to him so he bid them a fond fair-well and returned to his squad car. Sitting by the curb catching up on paperwork, some woman inquired as to why he allowed those young men to escape. Now, Murphy received the other side of the story. These young men were in the process of egging this woman's house when he interrupted them. Murphy explained that she never came out to speak to him, so he allowed the boys to go on their way.

He was not a bit concerned about the woman and her house, but he was certainly annoyed that he had been duped. Murphy started searching the area for the vehicle and his four little perpetrators. Recalling eggs on their vehicle, he surmised that they could be located in a local car wash or the nearest gas station using a hose. Bingo! About three blocks away, Murphy spotted the boys hosing off their car in a gas station. Backup cars arrived and these four hooligans were placed under arrest for disorderly conduct. Their automobile was parked legally on the side street.

Earlier in the shift, Murphy spoke to a couple of police women who had confiscated a case of eggs from a couple of young neighborhood pranksters. They were in the process of driving the district egging gang members when Murph called them. They cheerfully donated two dozen eggs to their good sergeant and returned to their mission. Murphy proceeded to distribute these eggs onto this parked auto. He locked the doors, and returned to patrolling the neighborhood.

SPRAY THE FRIGGIN DOG

Sergeant Murphy and half a dozen squad cars responded to a large disturbance on the street. Upon arrival, the commotion that was reported as a massive violent disturbance was actually a simple disagreement between a few seemingly non-violent individuals. It still had to be sorted out before the officers could leave. As the mediating officers attempted to placate those involved, the dog in the adjacent ward was barking up a storm. Very little could be heard over his baying and yapping. The fence guarding the dog's enclosure was extensive and walking away from the nuisance of the dog was impossible. The dog followed his boundary and kept up the incessant barking.

Peace was ultimately restored and those involved were allowed to depart. Murph and a few officers were alone. Murphy found a knothole in the wooden fence and pulled out his pepper spray. Wiggling his finger enticingly in the hole while simultaneously whistling in short bursts, he attempted to attract is canine nemesis. As the pooch approached, Murph took one last cautionary look around. Standing in the rear window watching intently was the dog's owner. She stood witness to Murphy's unethical plan to treat this pooch to a blast of pepper spray. The plan was abruptly cancelled and the pooch barked Murphy into his squad car while he made his getaway.

THE PROPER WAY TO ANSWER A PHONE

Standing at the desk in the 16th District, Sergeant Murphy observed an officer answer the phone. The caller was apparently some unknown deputy. From what he could hear, the call went something like this:

Officer: "Hello, what can I do for you?"

Deputy: "Officer, this is deputy XXX, that's no way to answer a police department telephone. You are supposed to answer it by saying hello, then state your name, what district you work at and then how may I assist you?"

Officer: "Deputy, do you know whom you are speaking with?"

Deputy: "No."

Officer: "Then go fuck yourself." Click, he hung up.

About three minutes later, the district commander raced to the desk and started yelling about phone answering protocol. The unnamed culprit never was identified.

CAPS GRAFFITI PROBLEM SOLVED

As a CAPS Sergeant, one of your responsibilities is to find a community problem and work it until it is reduced or eliminated. Murphy's trouble was that on his particular beat, there were no real issues. His lieutenant was on his ass to find an issue, write it up, and start working on solving it. Using a pre-printed form Murphy was supposed to describe the issue, and formulate a plan of action to eliminate the problem within a certain time frame.

Murphy submitted his plan of action about the graffiti on Higgins Avenue. There were orange symbols spray painted on the street, alongside the curb. He declared that he was going to eliminate this graffiti within one month's time. Murph devised a systematic plan of action, and directed the officers on the beat to carry it to fruition. Within the stated time frame, the graffiti was completely eradicated. His CAPS plan was a total success. Job well done!

As Paul Harvey used to say, "Here's the rest of the story." You see, the graffiti that Murphy observed actually was Streets and Sanitation marking a portion of the road for excavation. They were positioning a sewer connection and marked the street with orange paint where they were going to tear up the existing asphalt. They completed their project within the month, thus the CAPS problem was eliminated within that same month. It looked good on paper!

PARAMEDICS ARE POLICEMEN'S FRIENDS

After a doctor glued the cut behind his ear, Sergeant Murphy left the local hospital and headed back into his district. Earlier, he had responded to a burglar alarm at a factory that high winds had apparently set off. As he was walking back through the huge sliding chain linked gate, the wind picked up again and blew the gate off its rails. As the gate fell, it struck Murph behind the ear causing a small gash; thus, the trip to the hospital.

Murphy was back in the car and headed into the station to complete the necessary paperwork. A call was broadcast about a fight with a man bleeding profusely. Of course with his luck, Murphy's driving right past the location so he took the job in. Pulling up on the scene, he observed a group wrestling on the grass in front of an apartment building. As he got closer, he realized that one person was gushing blood from his sliced up face. This guy apparently had been pushed head first through a front door storm window. Interesting enough, he was the violent offender who would not stop fighting. Murphy called for paramedics and attempted to persuade this bleeding fool to relax until medical assistance arrived. He then fixed his sights on Murph and was intent on kicking his ass. After a short struggle with the drunk, Murphy managed to handcuff him. While they tussled on the front lawn, Murphy opened a small wound on his finger. It was pinched in the locking mechanism of the hand cuffs, as happens occasionally when you wrestle with someone. The arrestee was finally tired out and was lying quietly on the grass, turning it a crimson color. Murph was standing about five feet away with small beads of blood rolling off his injured finger, dropping to the sidewalk.

With red lights eliminating the sky, first on the scene were the paramedics. They pulled to the curb and jumped out of the rig with equipment bags in hand. Sprinting past the bleeder on the ground, the paramedic grabbed Murph's red-tipped finger. He started to compress the cut to stop the bleeding. Murphy alerted him to the fact that the arrestee was in far worse shape. The paramedic looked him in the eyes and calmly stated that he was important and when he was finished with Murph he would deal with the arrestee. Murphy was humbled, as well as proud. He always loved and respected paramedics.

THE PRESIDENTIAL VISIT

The president visited Chicago and sergeant Murphy was in charge of a detail of officers that were assigned to block off sections of the expressway. This was done so the presidential security detail could transport him safely back to O'Hare Airport. All district sergeants involved in this detail had about four to six officers blocking various entrance ramps of the Kennedy Expressway from downtown to O'Hare Airport. All overpasses would also be covered by Chicago police officers. When the lead car from the presidential security detail ordered that certain sections of the highway be sealed, the squad cars at their designated locations would pull their cars across the top of the entrance ramps. This prevented any traffic from entering the expressway. They were later notified to open traffic up when the presidential motor cade drove past. Simple. This expressway shutdown had occurred hundreds of times before without incident. Today was different.

One of the officers working this detail was the laziest police officer Murphy had ever encountered in his thirty-year police career. Murphy repeatedly checked on his location assuring that he was alert and in position. Murph informed his watch commander that all personnel were on post and they were waiting for the orders to shut down the highway.

Over the citywide radio channel came the orders to shut down the Kennedy Expressway from downtown toward the airport in increments of about four ramps at a time. As the presidential limousine got closer to the airport, more ramps would be shut down and this continued until the presidential procession approached Lawrence Avenue, location of Murphy's problem child. The closures order came and was repeated over the radio. It was repeated over and over again with more of a fever pitch. The presidential motorcade approached Lawrence Avenue. While traffic from the ramp bled onto the highway and into the motorcade, secret service security teams leading the motorcade curbed two vehicles. The first vehicle observed the black SUV swerve into them and recognized

225

something awry. They immediately pulled to the side of the Kennedy Expressway. The second vehicle, driven by an elderly couple was forced to the side of the expressway by a black SUV occupied with men dressed in suits and armed with machine guns.

Murphy responded to the scene posthaste to find the officer just then attempting to block the entrance ramp as he was ordered to do earlier. Asking for a reason for his inability to accomplish such a mundane task, he responded that his vehicle did not start; therefore he could not block the entranceway. Responding to why he did not report this on his radio he replied that his radio was not functioning. Murphy suggested that he could have visually observed the motorcade coming and made the cutoff simply by standing on the ramp waving his arms; he was confused at this proposition. At that point the radio blared and sergeant Murphy was directed into the 17th District to report to his watch commander post haste.

Murphy entered the watch commander's office to be greeted with a head nod by the lieutenant to have a seat. The lieutenant was on the telephone in what appeared to be a one way conversation. At one point, he held the receiver away from his ear and Murphy heard loud screeching from the earpiece filling the office with very colorful profanity. The deputy was demanding to know why the secret service was forced to curb two cars with machine guns drawn. The lieutenant stated he would call the deputy back with his oral report and hung up. The lieutenant requested that Murphy investigate the reason for the dereliction of duty, he simply responded by naming the officer involved. The watch commander immediately understood.

Murphy called the officer into the station and initiated the complaint registered investigation by taking control of his police radio. The battery was checked and determined to be sufficiently charged to allow the officer to use it without disruption. Using his radio, Murphy conducted a radio check on the two radio zones being used that day; both radio checks were loud and clear from the dispatchers. The radio worked well. Murphy then directed his attention to the officer's vehicle. Murphy called in an 'R man', a mechanic from the police garage that repairs police vehicles on the street. He inspected the officer's police vehicle and stated that the vehicle was in normal operating condition. There was no malfunction or disruption in the officer's vehicle.

The officer refused to give a statement and Murphy saw no reason for any other testing or interviews. The officer went home and Murph continued his investigation. After obtaining a complaint registered number against this officer for inattention to duty, Murphy submitted his initial reports and went home.

Sergeant Murphy witnessed the total humiliation of a deputy, as well as the profound denigration of the reputation of one of the country's best police departments. By the time Murphy arrived at work the next day, word of this colossal fuck-up had already filtered into every district in the city. Their district was the laughing stock of the department, and Murphy was writing the paper to punish the culprit who caused this embarrassment.

Generally, a completed complainant registered investigation would take weeks, even months to complete. Needless the say, this investigation was fast-tracked. Murphy had already documented his initial investigation about the proper working condition of the officer's radio and vehicle. His description of the vehicle was supported by the accredited statements of the R man. His attempts at the radio checks were documented when Murphy requested reports from the 911 dispatchers and copies of the tape recordings. And the most interesting aspect of this investigation was when Murphy made a visit to the deputy's office and spoke to his secretary. With a straight face Murphy demanded a report from the deputy documenting his involvement in this complaint registered investigation as the complainant. The startled sergeant/secretary finally realized why Murph needed the report and he informed him that he would have it without haste. Murphy smiled and turned down an offer to speak to the deputy in person and informed the sergeant that he would be watching the police mail.

The following day a crisp report was hand delivered to Murphy at the start of his shift. It detailed quite nicely the events from the day before. After a few days, Murphy submitted his investigation's findings, including his recommendation of disciplinary actions against the officer.

By now, the severity of the situation was diluted and jokes were being narrated throughout the station. Murphy submitted his final report containing about twenty pages of required information to the good lieutenant. In this investigation he found the officer to be guilty of rule violations in that he failed to obey a direct order and as such committed a dereliction of duty. The disciplinary action Murphy recommended was death. When the lieutenant read that portion of his report, Murphy thought he was going to fall off his chair. He looked at Murphy and agreed whole-heartedly with the recommendation, but instructed him to rewrite the report. Murphy had written two disciplinary portions and he took back the phony report and handed him the official copy. Murphy recommended three days off without pay and submitted the official report to the lieutenant, which he accepted with a smile.

The humiliation and embarrassment involved cost one Chicago police officer three days off without pay. It cost the City of Chicago dearly in status.

WORKING THE SYSTEM

A beat car in the 17th District was assigned a domestic disturbance call. Once they arrived, they requested sergeant Murphy to join them. As he left his squad car, Murphy was handed paperwork from the Cook County Court. It was a court order of protection, which declared that the woman's ex-boyfriend could not disturb her in any way. He could not communicate with her, nor can he be present at her residence or work place.

The ex-girlfriend was standing in front of the house she deserted one year earlier. Prior to the mutual breakup, she had moved into a house that the boyfriend owned. He was renovating the house at the time of separation. After not hearing from the ex-girlfriend for more than a year, he had moved on with his life. The house was almost fully remodeled, and a new girlfriend had just moved her furniture in and was residing there. His life was on the mend, until tonight.

A court order is an order from a judge that cannot be disputed anyplace but a courtroom. Whatever the order dictates, it must be followed out of fear of being held in contempt of court. This not only includes subjects of the court order, but also police officers who are obligated to enforce these faceless orders.

It was simple, she wanted the house. The nomadic ex-girlfriend apparently spoke to someone with the necessary knowledge to orchestrate this legal takeover. She misleads the court into believing the relationship was ongoing, and that she had been abused at the hands of this man. The court, attempting to protect domestic partners from abuse, drew up this order of protection.

At this point in time, the ex-boyfriend was informed that he would have to vacate the premises seeing that it was currently the ex-girlfriend's residence, and a judge ordered him not to be within two hundred feet of her. His current girlfriend was not mentioned in the court order; therefore she was allowed to stay if she chose to. The ex-girlfriend moved back in and the ex-boyfriend and his current girlfriend would be forced to find shelter elsewhere. He was advised to contact an attorney as soon as possible and initiate legal action to regain his house.

This is what is commonly referred to as a cluster fuck.

TASERS REALLY WORK

Responding to a request by officers to assist at a disturbance with a drunken woman, Murphy didn't understand why he was needed. He found out soon enough. Walking into the apartment, a disheveled woman who was barricaded in a corner looked at him and picked up a quart of whiskey and locked her lips onto it. She tipped it in the air and started to chug. When Murphy was younger he tended bar in various taverns across Chicago and had witnessed some championship chugging, but this woman was the indisputable queen. Murph stood in amazement as air bubbles continually rose inside the inverted bottle, as its contents spilled into her gullet. He allowed this to continue believing that dealing with a super drunk woman was less physically demanding than dealing with a slightly intoxicated one. After what seemed like eternity, she paused. Murphy's eyes followed her hand as she placed the near empty whiskey bottle on the table, and before anyone could react, she picked up a ten-inch Bowey knife that had escaped their view. Standing six feet away with the table between them, Murphy felt no immediate threat, so he unholstered his Taser instead of his .45 auto. He realized the woman was a threat to herself and not to the officers in the room. She turned toward Murphy and held the knife to her raised arm which showed signs of self-mutilation. Understanding one good slash could damage her beyond repair, he took aim with the Taser. After numerous commands to drop the knife, she started to cut herself. Murphy fired the two Taser darts into her and with a blood curdling scream she collapsed instantly. The table was hastily flipped to the side. Officer George kicked the knife across the floor and took control of it. Other officers handcuffed her just as paramedics walked through the doorway. After the initial jolt of 50,000 volts, the intoxicated young lady loaded her pants. Now, silent, intoxicated, and stinky, the paramedics strapped her onto a gurney. She regained her composure as she was being placed into the ambulance, and began to shout very nasty things at sergeant Murphy. Tasers are the next best thing to sliced bread.

DO AS I SAY, NOT AS I DO

Understanding how dangerous traffic chases are, and the propensity of the police brass to hang an officer, Sergeant Murphy dedicated a single roll call to this subject. At roll call, he informed all the officers that chases will not be tolerated. He further explained that there absolutely would be no chase unless a police officer got hurt and they were pursuing the offender. Murph exaggerated his position by stating that he didn't care if a nun got raped and the offender was fleeing. He didn't care if a squad car was sitting at an intersection and a car drove by and threw a baby out the window. There simply would be no traffic pursuits, car chases, or following a car at high speeds. Murphy dismissed roll call, got his radio and jumped into his squad car for a day of policing.

Ten minutes later Murphy was in pursuit of a vehicle wanted for armed robbery. Suburban police initiated the pursuit in their jurisdiction and chased the vehicle into Murphy's district where he picked up the pursuit. Now, leaving the district and running fifty miles an hour, Murphy pursued the car full of stick-up guys. The watch commander came on the radio and immediately called off the chase. Sergeant Murphy returned to the district with a chorus of reminders of his chase policy being repeated on the radio. He took a verbal beating for the next few days. Murph's only response was to laughingly say, "Do as I say, not as I do."

Bottom line, all the officers truly understood that his words to them about chases were meant to keep them safe. Police officers chase bad guys, like dogs chase cats. They often don't have the luxury of thinking things through due to the immediacy of the circumstances; police officers react instinctively.

THE CASE OF THE MISSING DRIVER'S LICENSE

Working as a midnight field supervisor, Murphy responded to a call of a large apartment building on fire. Being the middle of January and about three o'clock in the morning, it was freezing out. He was rushing to the scene with about a mile to go when he found himself behind a vehicle traveling at about fifteen miles per hour. To make matters worse, this guy had his left turn single on. Besides the siren blaring and the blue lights flashing, Murphy shined the spotlight in his rear window. Murphy couldn't take the chance of driving around him, just in case he did turn left. He was stuck. Cursing out loud and continuing to hit the siren and flash the spot light in his rearview mirror, Murphy traveled down Belmont Avenue at fifteen miles per hour. After a very painful couple of minutes, the slow-poke turned into the 14th District. Murphy quickly turned with him and curbed his vehicle. Murphy demanded his driver's license and once obtained, he ordered him to stay put. Jumping back into his squad, Murph tossed the driver's license into the glove compartment to be forgotten, so he thought.

Finally arriving at the scene of a fully engulfed apartment complex, Murphy requested further police assistance and two CTA busses for use as warming centers. He placed responding police units in the rear to block the alley. They shut down the street and used police vehicles as warming centers until the CTA buses arrived. The dispatcher alerted Murphy that he had a Plan Two in effect. A Plan Two consisted of about ten squad cars and a wagon. Being a new sergeant, he didn't fully realize the consequences of a Plan Two.

Standing in a river of ice and water, with semi-frozen fire hoses snaking down the street, Murphy spotted in the distance a tall figure walking toward his position. It was his watch commander. Murph hopped a couple of half-frozen puddles and went to meet him. As the watch commander approached, Murphy smiled and greeted him. It was immediately explained to Murphy that the watch commander had to respond to all Plan Twos. He asked Murphy if god died, and Murphy replied no. He turned and began to walk away, twisted his head toward Murphy and says if god died he should notify him and he would come back out. With that the watch commander returned to the warmth of the station. Murphy understood that he did not want to be out in the January cold watching an apartment building burn.

The fire department extinguished the fire and the CTA had all the occupants safely in warming busses. The Red Cross showed up and within a few hours, all displaced persons had adequate accommodations. "Board up" services were working feverishly and over the radio came an inquiry, "Does anybody in the 16th District have an individual's driver's license?" By now Murphy was exhausted and didn't feel like putting up with some drunk, and he certainly didn't want to pawn it off on any other police officer, so he kept his mouth shut. The fire trucks picked up hose and were gone; the city salt trucks were making Belmont Avenue drivable again. Murphy left to get a warm cup of coffee forgetting about the driver's license.

Weeks went by and sergeant Ricky griped to Murphy about a complaint registered investigation he was assigned to handle. It seemed that an unknown police officer stopped a driver a few weeks earlier and confiscated his driver's license. Ricky believed it was an officer from the adjoining district. Murphy immediately realized he was the culprit. He couldn't tell Ricky because he is such an honest and dedicated police sergeant and just knowing the truth would kill him. Murphy kept his mouth shut.

Time went by and Ricky kept Murph informed about the lack of progress in the investigation. While working the midnight shift, Sergeant Ricky was taking the complainant to view photos of police officers at the internal affairs office during the morning hours. Murphy had to bite his tongue when Ricky told him that, or Murph would have blown his cover. The complainant could not identify any officer as the one who took his driver's license. The investigation was finally closed because of insufficient evidence.

Ricky was driving his regular sergeant's car, the same car Murphy was driving when the license disappeared. By now, Murphy had finally been assigned to a regular car. The sergeants met one early morning and pulled their cars side by side and talked from car to car. Ricky told him about finally closing out this investigation from hell. He was visually agitated as he explained the entire process of failing to locate and identify the perpetrator of this driver license theft. When he was finished and had gotten this aggression off his chest, Murph asked him to open the glove compartment in his car and take a look. With a puzzled expression Ricky followed directions. Finding a driver's license inside, Murphy inquired if it was the complainants. He shouted, "Hell yeah!" Murphy explained the circumstances of how it got there and said he had that license in the glove box for the entire length of the investigation. Ricky laughed. Murphy laughed. Ricky mumbled something about killing Murphy and they both drove away.

IT PAYS TO BE NICE

It was a boring day in the 16th District with very few calls. This being the rare occasion that there was an abundance of sergeants working, so Murphy's jobs were few and far between. He was flagged down by a frazzled looking woman. She needed the directions to Midway Airport in order to pick up a family member. She was from a small town sixty miles north of Chicago. Flagging Murphy down, she was under the impression that Midway was just minutes away. He attempted to explain the various routes and she seemed to become more and more confused. Finally, Murphy just told her to follow him. They entered the Kennedy Expressway and headed south. She stayed on his tail, and as they exited, she followed Murph to the gates of the airport. With a wave and smile, she realized her goal, and Murphy headed back to his district on the far north side. Letting the dispatcher know that he was back from his journey, she informed Murph that he had missed nothing of relevance.

Weeks went by and Murphy received a letter from the Chicago Police Superintendent's office complimenting him on his actions involving a lost woman. Accompanying it, he also received a police shoulder patch and a very thoughtful note written by a police dispatcher from a small town north of Chicago. This was his lost woman. She never asked for privilege. She never requested special assistance. She was elated over the service she received in the big city, a memory she said she would never forget.

Sometimes it's the little things that are important.

A TRUE HERO

Being a sergeant working days in the 16th District Murphy responded to a curious call of an electric pole leaning over. Just west of Cicero Avenue he observed a group of people waving frantically. They were shouting directions to go to the alley. As he drove his squad down the street and slowly approached the alley, Murph observed what appeared to be an accident involving a bobcat, a construction digging machine. It was leaned up against a Commonwealth Edison pole in the alley, with its bucket fully extended. The electric pole was leaning and it appeared that the bobcat was preventing the pole from falling across the alley onto the nearby apartment building. To add urgency, the pole had a transformer attached to it. Speaking to the bobcat driver, Murphy deciphered the story.

A subterranean cable crew was burrowing an underground tunnel in order to run telecommunication cables. They tunneled too close to a Com Ed pole. The trenching destabilized the base of the pole, and it started to tip across the alley, aimed directly at a two story apartment building. As luck would have it, there was a construction crew digging a foundation for a building just down the alley. A young Mexican man was driving the bobcat and backfilling the newly poured foundation with stone, when he witnessed the commotion. Quick thinking saved the day. He drove the machine into the slowly leaning pole, raised the bucket and pushed with everything the powerful bobcat had. He forced the pole back into a safer position and locked the small machine into place. The bobcat secured the pole and averted a catastrophe. You see, it was a very warm July day, and if the transformer fell on the tarred roof, spilling the hot oil inside and with the sparks from the broken electric lines, disaster was simply moments away. Commonwealth Edison responded to Murphy's call of an emergency and a supervisor was on scene very shortly. He immediately requested the proper equipment that was redirected from another site. The pole was secured.

Murphy

Now for the rest of the story. Murphy was so impressed with the young Mexican who risked his life, he recommended him up for an award. Murphy wrote and re-wrote this act of bravery up four times and was repeated told that he was had to use a different form each time. Murphy used every damn form available and was still directed elsewhere. He was simply trying to do the right thing and draw attention to a person who risked his life to stave off a potential disaster. After months of running in circles, Murphy requested assistance from his district commander. Murph explained how he was being thoroughly discouraged by the people in the ivory tower downtown, and miraculously within days the DC accomplished what Murph couldn't do in months.

A beautiful wooden plaque was furnished, telling the hero's tale. At the next community meeting, the Chicago Police Department presented this plaque to the young man. He was greeted as the hero he was and stood proudly as an eloquent speech was delivered by the district commander. Beaming with pride, he accepted this token of gratitude from the City of Chicago. I'm sure this is a story has been recited, with pride, to his children.

WHY RUIN THEIR LIVES?

On the second day of being a sergeant in the 16ᵗʰ District, Murphy invited himself to a party that the tactical unit just raided. As he pulled to the curb, he tried to avoid the blue and red plastic cups that were blowing in the wind. Exiting the squad car, Murphy was somewhat surprised at the sight of about thirty, neatly dressed young men, with their hands on the red cedar fence. There were no tactical supervisors working that night, so Murphy was the supervisor in charge. He was briefed by a tact officer and informed that their district wagon was on the way, along with wagons borrowed from outlying districts. They were to transport these thirty juveniles into the district so they could be charged with underage drinking. The tact officer was very pleased with this large catch.

Murphy asked if they were aggressive toward the officers. The answer was no. He asked if any weapons or narcotics were found. The answer was no. Finally he asked if any of these kids smarted off or were disrespectful in any manner. The answer again was no.

Murphy went from one end of the line to the other, inquiring what schools these kids attended and what their fathers did for a living. The answers were; all the local high schools. The fathers were policemen, firemen, electricians, plumbers, and other blue-collar workers. No weapons were found, not even a knife. No drugs were found, not even a bag of weed. Not a smart-aleck in the group, all "Yes sirs" and "No sirs."

Murphy called the tact officer over and informed him of what he had seen and explained that he needed a more substantial reason for arrests, other than the drinking violation. The tact officer happily explained that there were thirty arrests and that his tact team would be set for the month. When Murphy inquired about the charges and future records these kids would have, he replied that the charges were only misdemeanors. No big thing.

The thought of an arrest for the sake of statistics nauseated Murphy. He informed the officer that no arrests were to take place. Murphy got on the radio and cancelled the wagons. He instructed the officers to have the kids clean up the area, every single plastic cup. After the area was spotless, including the neighbor's front yards, the partygoers would be on their way.

This did not sit well with a few of the officers on the scene, but sometimes a supervisor has to make a decision based on what is best for all involved. Murphy couldn't live with himself believing that he ruined the future employment opportunities of these kids for doing something that he did when he was their age.

DOMESTIC ON DEVON

A domestic disturbance was assigned to a beat car and Murphy was in the vicinity, so he decided to take a ride. A sergeant was supposed to take in at least one domestic disturbance per shift and log it. Murphy arrived before the assigned beat car and noticed a car parked on the front lawn with two men leaning on it. Out of caution he decided to stop short of the address and observe some more. A woman came running up to his car forcing him to get involved before he was prepared. She poured out a story of woe and backed it up with alligator tears. She related to Murphy that her boyfriend and his friend were being abusive towards her. Murph approached the two men with carefully after they had been described as vicious, drunken, thugs. The beat car pulled up and they spoke to the two young men, who were actually respectful and surprisingly sober for that late hour. They had a quiet conversation about how this one young man had just thrown his drunken girlfriend out of the apartment for cheating on him. He explained in a very calm and civilized manner that he and his out-of-town buddy were sitting in the apartment having a beer when his live-in girlfriend came home. She was drunk and belligerent. She had been out with another man and attempted to start an argument with him. She eventually infuriated him with tales of her infidelity, and he finally threw her out. After being removed from the apartment, the girlfriend became furious and drove his automobile onto the front lawn. She then called 911 to report domestic abuse believing that the police would immediately take her side, arrest the boyfriend, and tow his prized possession. Listening intently for about five minutes, Murphy excused himself and went to the front door to speak with the girlfriend, who had secretly snuck around him and entered the apartment.

By now more officers arrived so Murph felt comfortable leaving the officers with two men. He rang the apartment doorbell and announced himself as the police officer she had spoken with earlier. This young lady answered the apartment intercom with a "Go fuck yourself." Murph had the female version of Dr. Jekyll and Mr. Hyde. She not only refused to allow him entry, but she called him some of the nastiest names imaginable. Murph realize he had been played for a sucker. The boyfriend, with his house keys left inside, now requested that officers forcibly enter his apartment. Murphy explained that the police cannot do such a thing without reasonable cause and locking yourself out of your own apartment does not justify the police making a forced entry. The girlfriend was now at the front window on the second floor laughing and taunting the boyfriend and the police. Reasonable conversation has turned to ridicule with the girlfriend pouring on the abuse. Murphy was beside himself because he allowed this to happen and he never saw it coming.

Murphy explained to the boyfriend that the most amenable way to handle this situation was for him and his friend to get a motel room for the night and return in the morning. It took a great amount of convincing, but he finally agreed. Murphy requested that the girlfriend in the second floor window pass down his wallet so he can leave. Instead, she launched the contents of his wallet into the air and laughingly watched them flutter to the ground. She took his money out of his wallet, hung it out the window and teased him, then put in into her bra. Overjoyed, she tossed his now empty wallet from the second story window onto the lawn below. The police stayed around long enough for the boyfriend to gather his papers.

Ten minutes later police responded back to the scene, this time a call of a noise disturbance. Murphy approached the boyfriend and he was livid because he didn't do anything wrong and he was the one being punished. Murphy again explained that he wished things were different, but he would have to go. For the second time he left.

Minutes later, there was a radio broadcast of a man with a knife at the same location. With blue lights activated and siren screaming, the street in front of the two-flat was jammed with squad cars. The boyfriend was sitting in the back seat of a squad car handcuffed. The girlfriend was upstairs with her new boyfriend being interviewed by a responding officer. It seemed that the girlfriend invited the new boyfriend over and then called the old boyfriend to tell him that they were going to have sex on his bed in his apartment. The old boyfriend returned with a knife and kicked the apartment door in threatening the new boyfriend. No injuries occurred, just a lot of shouting, but for this he was immediately arrested and placed in the squad car.

All was calm. But, Murphy recalled being duped into feeling sorry for this young lady and eventually being played a fool. He remembered the "Go fuck yourself" and the other unpleasantries that were bestowed on him and his fellow officers. Murphy re-interviewed the now soft-keyed young woman. With her smooth demure voice, she once again was a friend of the police. Murphy stationed a police officer with her and directed him not to let her out of his sights for any reason.

He returned to the arrested boyfriend in the squad car and asked him if he would like to sign complaints against the girlfriend for theft of his money from the earlier dispute. He stated he would be thrilled to do so. He had the handcuffs removed long enough to sign a complaint against his girlfriend for taking money from his wallet. Murphy returned to the apartment where the young lady was schmoozing with the officer left to guard her. Murphy requested that she be handcuffed and read her Miranda Rights. She was placed under arrest for theft. The crying began, and quickly turned into verbal attack aimed at Murphy, interspersed with some high pitched cursing. The boyfriend was pleased that she was going to jail, but not as happy as sergeant Murphy was.

TASING KARATE JOE

In police work, it pays to be prepared for the unexpected. While Sergeant Murphy was assigned to the 17ᵗʰ District, Sergeant Jack and he were directed to present a table-top exercise for local school principals. This presentation involved completing a practice exercise that consisted of duplicating a scenario of a gas main break in front of a school. They discussed evacuation and safe keeping of the students. They made use of the brand new conference room in the 16ᵗʰ District. Coffee and pastries were served. Principals and assistant principals from the local schools were gathered around a circular group of tables, with sergeants Jack and Murphy situated at the top.

As the first slide was lighting up the screen, Murphy remembered looking at a Catholic nun taking notes and listening intently. Then the blaring screams of a "10-1" broke the tranquil setting. Both sergeants instantly stared at one another and turned their radios up while stepping away from the table. The shouts on the radio were alarming but still the location could not be made out. They could hear a serious struggle taking place and then finally an officer shouted, "The rear of 16." Murphy stepped out of the conference room and looked down the long hall and was astonished to see two police officers in a deadly struggle with a shirtless arrestee. Jack and Murphy raced toward the commotion and joined in the struggle. After a few seconds of rolling around on the station floor, Murphy shouted "Taser! Taser! Taser!" This warning allowed the officers involved to know that he was going to shock the arrestee with the Taser. The wagon crew rolled off the pile and Jack and Murph dry stunned the warrior.

Dry stunning means that they pressed the Taser on various muscles of his body and ran 50,000 volts of electricity through him causing what is commonly referred to as a 'Charlie Horse'. This causes the muscles in the body to constrict.

Jack and Murph were literally nose to nose using their combined weight to attempt to control this muscular young man while each infused

50,000 volts into his torso. With the smell of burnt flesh and understanding that they were ultimately losing this battle, Murphy call out to Jack, "Let's tase him." They both rolled off on either side of their opponent and simultaneously fired two Taser darts into his now sweaty body. With fifteen police officers now standing around them in a circle, like a fight in grammar school, Jack and Murph pumped electricity into the subject all the while shouting instructions for him to give up. Understanding that there is no such thing as giving up in martial arts, the subject fought on and the sergeants continued to pump more and more voltage into his now smelly body. After a total of thirteen or fourteen tasings, the subject finally went limp. The surrounding officers jumped in and re-handcuffed him while applying leg irons. They carefully dragged him to a waiting cell. Fire department paramedics were called and they removed the Taser's barbs from the arrestee's skin declaring the subject in no need of any further medical assistance. The subject eventually fell asleep from exhaustion.

The sergeants later found out that the arrestee was a martial arts instructor and had been abusing steroids for months. That morning, he went into a rage and beat his mother quite savagely. At the scene of arrest, he was calm and followed police direction without incident. He was arrested and handcuffed behind his back and placed in the wagon for transport to the district. During the ride, the arrestee slipped the handcuffs in front of him. When the transporting officers observed this they took due diligence in walking him into the rear door of the station, one officer attached to each of his arms. The arrestee was calm and composed when he entered the police station. But once inside the door, he pulled away kicking one officer in the side of the face and head butting the second one, knocking both to the ground. The fight was on and the "10-1" was broadcast over the police radio. This is when Jack and Murphy got involved.

After taking turns attending to the required paperwork, while still completing the emergency scenario, Jack and Murph dismissed their meeting. The exercise was cut short, but still completed, and those principals involved left the 16th District with a story to remember.

SOMETIMES IT'S THE LITTLE THINGS

Almost all the officers that worked in the district parked their personal cars in a grocery store's parking lot across from the station. Every night, about fifteen minutes before the end of the tour, Sergeant Murphy assigned a squad car from the midnight shift to sit in the parking lot. Being an exceptionally cold month, this allowed the officers on the afternoon shift an opportunity to start their personal vehicles and let them warm up while checking off. The 911 dispatcher and Murphy had been bumping heads for the past few weeks over what she called was improper use of police personnel. Murphy not so delicately, explained that he was in charge of the street and her job was to answer phones and dispatch jobs. She took this issue to her boss who inquired if Murphy's watch commander was aware of this inappropriate misuse of manpower. Under questioning from his watch commander, Murphy responded that he monitored the radio at all times and there were always sufficient cars available to answer all 911 calls. This was a brutally frigid winter and what little they could do for the troops was easily justified in Murphy's mind. His watch commander agreed that Sergeant Murphy was the street supervisor and he assigned cars the way he saw fit. The afternoon officers continued to drive home in warm vehicles.

BOUNTY ON GANG MEMBERS

Sergeant Murphy caught wind of some very disturbing news one day while having coffee at the local donut/coffee shop. It seems that the leader of a local gang, around Lawrence and Kedzie, harassed and embarrassed one of the new recruits by menacing him at the scene of a fire. The recruit was assigned to control pedestrian traffic at an alley during a very large apartment fire in order to allow the fire personnel to do their work. The gang leader, being drunk, challenged the new officer to a fight in front of a crowd of dozens of people, calling him a pussy and other foul names. Being brave because he was dealing with a recruit who was unsure of how to handle this type of situation, he continued to belittle and disparage this young man.

The following day at roll call, Sergeant Murphy put a bounty on the heads of all members of this local gang. He explained to the officers on the shift, that whoever arrests one of these gang members, for any reason, would get one hour off the end of his tour of duty. Any police officer that arrests the leader would get the full remainder of the tour of duty off, no questions asked. The only catch was that Murphy had to be notified of all arrests. Officers Terry and Jack, two of the district's most aggressive officers, sprinted out the door and quickly returned to the station with six shitheads stacked double in the back seat of their squad car. They received six hours off the remainder on their tour. Murphy notified his watch commander who smiled and applauded the tenacity displayed in handling the situation.

In the following few day, officers would rush out of roll call and hit the street even before their tour of duty officially started. Murphy explained to every thug arrested that he was arrested because his leader disrespected a Chicago police officer and the police would continue to do so. Arrests of gang members rose and after a few days officers Terry and Jack struck gold: they arrested the leader. Murphy was notified and he came into the station to visit him and explained that they would continue to arrest his fellow gang members because of his disrespect of the fellow officer. Asshole complained that his constitutional rights were being violated. Murphy slid next to him on the hard metal bench and put his arm around his shoulder. Murph lied to him as he cheerfully explained that he would go in front of a judge and swear that asshole put a gun to Murph's head and pulled the trigger with it misfiring. Murphy explained that the accompanying charge would be attempted murder of a police officer and he would receive thirty years in the penitentiary. "Don't ever fuck with our police officers."

Murphy's plan was working fantastically well and, as an unintended consequence, the drug sales in the district were diminished greatly. The gang banging dealers hid during Murph's tour of duty, the drug corners had nobody to work them and eventually dried up.

The gang leader was shot and killed about a week later in a dispute. It seemed that someone in his gang didn't appreciate his alleged involvement in another gang member's murder.

YOU DA MAN!

The radio blared: "Man with a gun." All available police officers headed to the scene. The radio broadcast included information about a man who had just threatened someone with a gun and then vanished into the residential neighborhood. It was dusk and his clothing description was very general. Murphy drove the side streets and looked for signs of the offender. Another supervisor, Sergeant Joe surveyed the dark street and viewed a young man sitting on the front stairs of an unlit house. This young man was sweating profusely and his heart was beating like a drum. The sergeant collected this fellow, walked him back to the street and ordered him to place his hands on the squad. All was going according to plan when, with cat-like reflexes, the subject pushed off against the car and bounced back into the sergeant, while shouting "Fuck you bitch!" Next, he was sprinting down the sidewalk with the sergeant in foot pursuit. At this point it's no contest, between the young stud in his prime with the old-time sergeant. Out of nowhere, a figure was sprinting alongside the sergeant. The Good Samaritan inquired, "Do you want me to get him for you?" The sergeant, naturally replied "Yes." With that, the mysterious savior jetted away, leaped and caught the offender in mid-air attempting to scale an eight-foot chain link fence. The Good Samaritan grabbed hold and body slammed the evader into the ground, bouncing his head off the pavement. The sergeant handcuffed the stunned thug. As he regained consciousness after the initial shock, he looked up at the only person around, the sergeant and said, "You da man." The Good Samaritan was nowhere to be found. The sprinter was now arrested. While in the district he screamed and cursed every officer he came in contact with, with the exception of sergeant Joe, the guy who he thought took him down. When his eyes met the silver-haired sergeant, with the look of admiration, he repeated, "You da man!"

Rest in peace Joe.

ACKNOWLEDGMENTS

I hope you enjoyed Murphy's thirty plus years of police stories. I wrote this book with honesty about the real police officers working the streets of Chicago. Police officers are real people: fathers, mothers, sisters and brothers. Police officers are: carpenters, lawyers, family counselors, drug advisors, chauffeurs, firemen, race car drivers, dog trainers, doctors, wrestlers and boxers, peace keepers and soul-less survivors, and so much more.

Police officers bleed and cry, their bones break causing the same pain that all people feel. They mow their lawns, change diapers and flat tires. They catch the flu and sneeze and cough like other people. They drink too much on occasion and sometimes argue with their loved ones. Officers are also emotionally drained from the horrifying jobs they handle. It hurts to see their families attacked at schools and at workplaces by ignorant people and the constant news barrage of negativity. Yes, police officers, as cool and constrained as they are, do have emotions buried deep beneath the skin. Not often do they release these feelings, but when they do come out, life is usually changed forever.

What makes a police officer different from other people is that they run toward gun fire. They see trouble and without consideration of themselves, they react. Police officers are always vigilant and always prepared to do battle. They race to the scene where normal people are racing to get away from. Police are a different breed, and I am proud to say I was one of them.

I salute my brothers and sisters in blue. With honor and dignity bestowed upon them all, I dedicate these writings to them. In particular, I salute those fine men and women who have left us for another world. I have had the honor of knowing and working with the best that God placed on earth. Rest in peace officers. And to all still serving and protecting, stay safe and go home tonight.

SPECIAL ACKNOWLEDGEMENTS

I thank my wife Sandy for putting up with thirty years of doubt, worry, and lost days. I thank my sons Nick and Chris for putting up with a police man for a father, and all that goes along with that.

GLOSSARY OF DEFINITIONS

911 Operator

The police radio operator who dispatches calls for police
service to the police as in the field

10-1.

Emergency radio broadcast that a police officer needs help

10-4.

Acknowledge a radio dispatch as a two person unit

10-99.

Acknowledge a radio dispatch as a single person unit

22 cal

A .22 caliber bullet or a weapon that fires a .22 cal bullet

38 cal

A .38 caliber bullet or a weapon that fires a .38 cal bullet

45 cal

A .45 caliber bullet or a weapon that fires a .45 cal bullet

357

A .357 caliber bullet or a weapon that fires a 357 cal bullet

Aggravated battery.

A crime that involves serious injury or dangerous weapon

Bonafide.

When a dispatched job is authentic

CAPS.

Chicago Alternative Policing Strategies

Cabrini Green.

A Chicago public housing project

CFD.

Chicago Fire Department

City-wide.

Radio broadcast that is heard city-wide, over-rides all zones

Civilian dress.

Regular street clothes instead of a uniform

CTA.

Chicago Transit Authority

Code the job.

Give a number code explaining the disposition of the assignment

CPD.

Chicago Police Department

C R number

A complaint registered against a police officer

Crime Lab.

Specialized forensics investigators used on major incidents

CTA.

Chicago Transit Authority

Bobcat.

A small digging machine

DEA.

Drug Enforcement Agency

Dog cage.

A cage in the police station for storing stray animals

Domestic.

A police disturbance between persons residing together

Disregard.

Radio broadcast when no further units are needed on the scene

Dry stun.

Putting the Taser on a person=s muscle and sending 50,000 volts of electricity through the muscle causing a cramp.

E.T.

Evidence Technician. A specially trained officer that collects forensic evidence from crime scenes

FBI.

Federal Bureau of Investigation

FTO.

Field Training Officer, An officer who trains recruits in the district

General Orders.

Regulations of the Chicago Police Department

Home invasion.

A robbery taking place in a residence.

Ivory Tower.

The nick-name for police headquarters

Inspector.

A police lieutenant that ensures that officers abide by the rules set by the Chicago Police Department

Light bar.

The horizontal bar on top of the police vehicles that hold the blue lights, siren, and fog horn

Mars lights.

The blue lights on top of the police vehicles

Movers.

Traffic citations for a moving violation

P. A.

Public announce system in the squad car

Paper.

The police report

Paper car.

Unit assigned to write the report

PCP.

Also known as Angel Dust, An animal tranquilizer ingested by people for the hallucinogenic properties

Recruit.

An officer during training

Rocks.

A concrete path along Lake Michigan in Chicago

Slim-jim

A tool used to open locked car doors

Special employment.

A police officer working his day off for the CTA

Specialized unit.

A group of police officers that specialize in a particular area of police work. Examples; narcotics, gangs, traffic.

Tactical unit.

A specialized group of police officers that work in civilian dress and unmarked squad cars

Taser.

A less than lethal handheld pistol like device that police use to stun combative individuals by shooting two electric barbs into them and conveying 50,000 volts of electricity causing muscle cramps

The air.

Access to the radio zone without interference from other officers

Radio priority.

No one else talks on the radio until the ongoing emergency is over

Radio Zones,

The entire Chicago police radio system is broken into sections called zones.

Normally each zone has two districts on it. This allows smooth communication.

Rank by appointment

Deputy

Commanding officer in charge of a large element of police officers

District Commander

Commanding officer in charge of a police district

Watch Commander

A commanding officer in charge of a watch in a police district

Captain

A commanding officer usually a district commander

Rank by testing

Lieutenant

A watch commander, a field lieutenant, or commanding officer in charge of a specialized unit

Sergeant

Normally in charge of a group of street officers

Detective

Does follow-up investigations

FTO, Field Training Officer

A police officer who trains recruits in the district

Police officer or beat officer

A police officer assigned to a particular area in the district to patrol

Watch.

A shift in police jargon

Printed in the United States
By Bookmasters